Alice

Dying is simple.
It's coming back when things get interesting.

John Knight

Published in 2021 by FeedARead.com Publishing.
A Modfiction imprint.

Book and cover design by John Knight. Final interior by the author.

This is a work of fiction. Names, characters, businesses, places, events,
locales, and incidents are either the products of the author's imagination or
used in a **fictitious** manner. The Crossley & Porter staff mentioned within the
novel are entirely fictious. Any resemblance to actual persons, living or
dead, or actual events is purely **coincidental.** Celebrities, singers, bands,
groups are mentioned in their historic real time appearances.

Also, by John Knight

Jimmy Mack
(Some kind of wonderful)

The Jimmy Mack 1967 trilogy:

1 Strong Love (Side A)

2 Let The Good Times Roll (Side B)

3 The New Breed

Dedicated to Bill Williams.
Writing Alice would have been so much harder without our chats.

And to my daughter,
Kimberley-Joy Knight (1984-20~~16~~21)

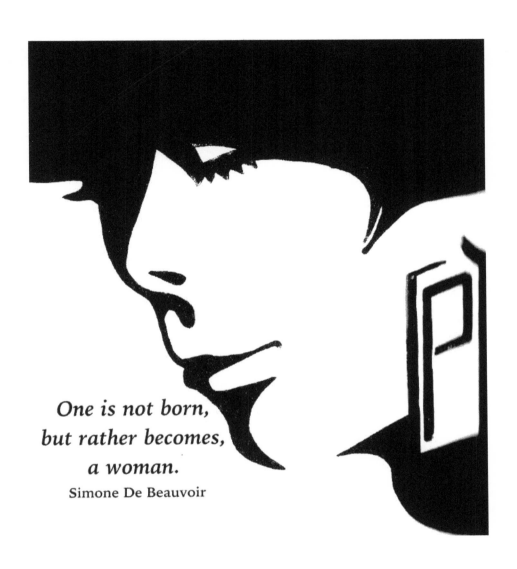

One is not born,
but rather becomes,
a woman.

Simone De Beauvoir

"When I used to read fairy-tales, I fancied that kind of thing never happened, and now here I am in the middle of one! There ought to be a book written about me, that there ought! And when I grow up, I'll write one—but I'm grown up now," she added in a sorrowful tone, "at least there's no room to grow up any more here."

Lewis Carroll – Alice in Wonderland

Foreword

Before her deliberate disappearance, Alice Liddell left a sealed package in my safekeeping. The parcel came with clear and precisely dated instructions as to when I should open it. My first thought assumed this was another one of her novels. There were further detailed instructions. No one should read this manuscript other than her closest friends: Hester Clayton, James and Effy MacKinnon, and me. Afterwards, we four would have to decide if her siblings, Edie, and Frank should read the manuscript. Failing an agreement, we four would have to make a final agreed and binding decision irrespective of her siblings' wishes. Should the manuscript be published?

Naturally, as instructed, I began to read the text. The more I read, the more I kept wondering if there could be any truth to Alice's strange revelations? Was this a novel? Or an autobiographical hoax? Was Alice playing some weird practical joke on her closest friends and family as she disappeared from our lives?

A celebrated Sixties fashion model Alice Liddell was a founding member of the famed New Breed collective. At the peak of her career, she retired from modelling at twenty-five, much to everyone's surprise. The next five years saw her continue to manage and mentor a younger generation of fashion models. Alice also assisted in the running of the New Breed modelling agency while at the same time writing the first of her three best-selling novels. **The Reincarnation of Maisie Miller** *was the first to be published.* **The Transmigration of Souls (A Hypothesis),** *a non-fiction work, followed.*

Alice remains one of my dearest friends. Seven days separated our physical arrival in the world. It appears we knew another almost from birth. Our mothers met and befriended one another on the hospital's maternity ward. Their friendship led to Alice and me growing up together as friends in our own right. We attended the same primary school and later the same grammar school. As little children and as schoolgirls, the two of us were inseparable. When adolescence and puberty reared its head, our relationship changed for a short time.

My immature involvement at fourteen with a man in his twenties left me in an emotional mess. I had made the terrible mistake of leaving school to work as a Chemist's assistant to please him. With my mother's life disintegrating from increasing bouts of severe depression, her friendship with Alice's mother faltered. Around the same time, Lorna Liddell's husband died, leaving her with Alice and two other siblings to bring up. Our friendship waned for a while as we all attempted to sort out our lives.

An accidental meeting with her sister upset me as I learned what had happened to Alice. After a sudden near-lethal collapse, she had lost all recollection of her previous life. Alice was unable to remember or recognise anyone, not even me. We all hoped in time her memory would return. It never returned entirely, if it ever did at all. When we did meet again, Alice's personality had changed completely. I did not know who she was, even though she possessed the same familiar physical likeness. Alice had changed so much she had become someone else, someone entirely different. We renewed our friendship despite the strange change. I know, looking back, it was the best thing we two ever did. Our closeness has remained bound and entwined throughout our lives.

After reading the manuscript, my immediate reaction made me question who Alice really was? Was this supposedly autobiographical account a practical joke? If it was a practical joke, then it was an elaborate one. Alice had a great sense of humour, but not one where I could imagine her going to so much trouble to play a simple prank. I confess she has left me wondering. Some days I dismiss it as an elaborate, fanciful hoax, an indulgent, delicious joke perpetrated by my friend. Then there are days when I think what I've read cannot be anything but true.

Angie Thornton

Chapter 1

We'll Meet Again – Vera Lynn (Decca F.7268 – 1939)

Sunday 24 September 1966

The disbelief on my daughter's face was no surprise. It could be nothing less. Against reason, Cathy realised this was not some hideous hoax. Somehow the impossible had to be true. Less than fifteen minutes after opening the door to this unknown teenage girl, her mind must have reeled from my intimate disclosures.

The young woman who confronted her knew things only her father could know, but he was dead. He had died. She had attended his funeral. Yet here I was telling her about things only he could have known.

I knew all about the broken milk bottle. That was why I had made a point of recounting it as one of our many father-daughter shared secrets. Only the two of us knew about this incident.

Ivy had sent Cathy on an errand to the corner shop to buy a bottle of pasteurised milk. Six-year-old Cathy had let the milk bottle slip from her grasp as she stumbled on the doorstep outside the shop. I happened to be returning home when I came across my little girl in tears. Utterly distraught, she was staring at the shattered bottle watching the white liquid flow into the gutter.

1

My wife never found out, and Cathy never received a scolding. I did what any father would do and bought a replacement. Before reaching home, I wiped away her tears and made it our little secret.

"Ask yourself this, Cathy. How else could I know about the milk bottle and all the other things I've mentioned? Before today, we had never met." Cathy shook her head, her mousey brown wavy hair moving with the motion of her head.

As Phil Manley, I had never even met Alice Liddell or her family before I died. Nor had I even known of their existence.

"You live on the other side of Halifax from me. We attend different schools, and you have never had any previous connection with me before today. Yet here I am, Alice Liddell, who knows so many things about you. Ask yourself again, how can this be possible?"

With some trepidation, I had decided to seek out my family from a life I no longer had.

"Alice Liddell?"

"Except there no longer is an Alice Liddell. She's gone, and I'm her." I paused, giving her a moment or two to absorb my words. "There is no easier way to explain this to you."

So, I began to recount my bizarre tale.

"I came around to find myself dead." Pausing, I could see the words made no sense. There was no going back, so I pressed on. "When I discovered I was still alive but in someone else's body, it was worse. Much worse. Alice Liddell died at the same time I did. On the way to the mortuary, she came back from the dead. Except it wasn't Alice. It was me, your father."

"So how did you…come back…to life? What happened?"

I continued with my strange tale. "The pain stopped. For a moment it was as though I was falling down a dark hole. Then nothing. No awareness. Nothing. Suddenly, I was struggling to breathe. As my eyes opened, I found my face covered. So, I pulled aside the sheet covering my face and stared at a sterile white corridor ceiling. I was moving, shivering uncontrollably and feeling icy cold. With unbelievable speed and force, gasping for air and juddering violently, I sat up. The hospital gurney carrying me came to a sudden stop. My unexpected return to consciousness terrified the two mortuary attendants. It didn't do me much good either.

I'd seen fear in men's eyes during the fighting in France, North Africa, and Italy. The fear in the eyes of the mortuary men was of a different kind. They had blanched instantly, recoiling in horror, slowly freezing on the spot

2

in petrified shock. I'd seen men quake with fright during battle. The two men showed the same fear but without the quaking."

"What's going on? What's happening?" I demanded, gasping for air, my voice sounding peculiar.

When their initial shock and fear drained away, one of them stuttered. "You're supposed to be dead. We were taking you to the mortuary."

"Do I look dead?" It was all I could think to say, as I tried to work out what was happening.

"I'm surprised they didn't die of heart attacks," Cathy commented in a hushed awed tone, a slight shudder passing through her. "I would have soiled myself if it had been me and probably passed out too. So, what happened next?"

"They had me back in the ward before I could work out what was happening. At this stage, I hadn't yet realised what was going on. The doctor who had pronounced me dead less than half an hour earlier was also in shock as he returned. So were the nurses, who later told me my resuscitation was nothing less than miraculous."

In fact, the doctor had not been as thorough as he should have been. When he checked my vital signs, I was supposedly clinically dead. No pulse or heartbeat. I should have been biological dead when I revived and beyond resuscitation. Mysteriously my heart must have started beating after his cursory checks. So, probably my return from the dead was not quite so medically mysterious. Back in the ward, the doctor was considerably more thorough and puzzled by my unexpected revival.

When he began performing his checks, I became aware something was definitely not right with me."

"Like what?"

"He kept addressing me as Miss, then Alice. Why do you keep calling me Alice? I asked, bewildered. That's not my name. By now, it was becoming clear not everything was as it should be. When the stethoscope came out, I realised it was not. As the hospital gown parted, my breasts became exposed. Tiny as they were, they were not those of a man."

Cathy's eyes narrowed into slits as I paused.

"It wasn't just the sight of the female bust. I had a growing awareness my voice sounded strange: softer, higher-pitched, distinctly female, nothing like my baritone. Then there was the thick, long honey-coloured hair, not the short greying brown with the expanding bald patch of a man approaching

3

fifty. That was when it became clear to me. Somehow I had undergone a drastic physical change."

Entranced by my account, Cathy prompted. "So, what happened next?"

A tiny laugh issued from me, my feminine soprano voice still sounding unusual in my head. "I said something like, I can't believe this! I've turned into a woman. What have you done to me?"

"What did the doctor say to you?"

"He asked me if I had started my periods. If I had, then I was well on my way to womanhood at seventeen. That was when I burst out, saying I was a man, not a woman. For the first time since his failed diagnosis of my death, his worried serious expression cracked as though from relief. He chuckled, shaking his head, permitting himself a smile as he explained. It appeared I did not qualify as a man since I lacked the manly dangly bits between my legs. And that's what I became aware of next. My manhood was missing. What the doctor said next to the Ward Sister led me to make a snap decision. When he suggested a psychiatrist should check on my mental state, that settled it."

Before continuing, I took a deep breath as I recalled the scene in the hospital. "Momentary panic had gripped me when I heard the doctor's words. I made an instantaneous decision. If I was indeed in a female body, having displaced its owner, saying nothing would be a smart idea. Getting sectioned and placed in a mental institution would not be a clever move. Before any more words left my lips, I needed to find out what had happened to me. If this was a bad dream, I should have woken up by now. But this was no bad dream. The sounds, the smells, and touch experiences confirmed I was very much awake in a strange new reality."

I paused again. It gave me a moment or two to decide if I should tell her how I died. The decision was not easy, but I concluded I had no choice. My account would only serve to strengthen the truth of my story. My death had been painful. So too was my telling of how I had collapsed. The vivid recollection of the agonising pain remained. I kept it brief.

"The bar staff in the Upper George pub must have called for an ambulance. I remember an ambulance man peering in my face. My last thought before everything crashed to blackness was thinking I might get through this and survive. This did not prove the case." Grimacing, I sighed, recalling my last moments as Phil Manley.

Cathy nodded, tears forming as she listened to my words. The Upper George was where her father had suffered his heart attack in town. She knew

4

the pub's exact location. The Plebeians, where she went most Saturday nights, was in the same Victorian yard.

"Honestly, I had no choice but to do what I did after I came around. I had to get to grips with the situation in which I found myself. The threat of a psychiatrist checking on my mental state raised instant fears. The possibility of being sectioning for craziness seemed real. My Uncle Albert had been sectioned. They had never let him out after they took him away. It had been tantamount to imprisonment without trial. I was not going to let that happen to me. There was no way I dared to repeat what I had said to the doctor. All I could think was that I, Phil Manley, was now in a woman's body. The last thing I needed was to be sedated and to find myself in a padded cell like Uncle Albert. You have to understand my decision. To say nothing further was to survive the situation. For the time being, I would become Alice, whoever Alice had been. What else could I do?"

Cathy nodded in agreement as she deliberated my reasons for saying nothing more at the time.

"So, pretence had to be, and has to be, the key to lock the door on who I was," I offered pensively. "Which was why I have to keep pretending I've lost my memory and why I don't remember anything, except that my name is Alice."

"Do you have any of her memories?"

"Nothing. Not a thing. When she died, the girl left her body empty. It seems I got vacant possession with no information about who she was or her life."

"So, what happened next?"

"Perhaps the most difficult experience of all. Meeting Alice's mother, sister, and brother. They had begun grieving their loss and had not even managed to leave the hospital when they found themselves called back. I can't begin to describe their joy at seeing Alice reprieved from death. I felt and still feel awful about deceiving them. What else could I do?"

I hesitated as I recalled what had taken place next. "The reunion had been traumatic. Blubbering, tears, hugs, I found it a trying experience. They were all strangers. Faces I had never seen, persons I had never met. The worst part was seeing their expressions when I uttered the words, I'm sorry. I don't know who you all are. The look on the woman's…my mother's face was heart-rending."

The next part of the tale was a struggle to tell, as I remembered the heart-breaking memory of what was spoken. Word for word, this girl's mother,

5

Lorna, said, "Alice, it's me, your mother. How could you not know me, love? They are your sister and brother, Edie and Frank. Surely you know us?"

This stranger, her eyes red from weeping had lit briefly with joyful hope, only to become fearful once more. The look in her eyes on hearing the words I had spoken have haunted me since. Though she was a stranger, we made a compelling umbilical connection in a fraction of a second. For this woman's sake, I knew I would have to accept being Alice, at least for a while. She was going to be my surrogate mother. Like it or not, I would have to pretend to be her daughter. It was as though I had a supernatural obligation to do the right thing beyond any rational explanation.

Cathy immediately grasped my situation as I explained it and sympathised.

I had never been religious, having gone along with the usual C of E conformity. The brutality I witnessed on the battlefields shed me of any existing illusions about a God of peace and love. Yet, something had given me this second chance at life. A life I would not have otherwise but for this woman's loss of her child. How else could I explain my cruel miracle? Supernatural intervention or not, as Phil Manley, I had to accept my fate. There seemed no sane alternative to do otherwise.

How my new existence was going to work out, I had no idea. Here I was, a middle-aged man in a young woman's body. Adapting so unexpectedly and so suddenly to a new life was not only confusing, but it was also daunting. What other realistic choice did I have?

Phil Manley's premature death was my fault. I had squandered my life. Confessing this to Cathy was part penance, part plea for help. There was no one else to whom I could turn. My daughter was the only one I could trust with the predicament I now found myself living. My conversation with Cathy stopped short as we heard the front door opening. Ivy had returned from shopping sooner than I expected. For a brief instant, I feared she would see through me. A stupid thought, even as she looked me over. I was no longer Phil Manley, at least not physically. But then, who was I?

*"It's no use going back to yesterday,
because I was a different person then."*

Lewis Carroll (Alice in Wonderland)

Chapter 2

If I Could Live My Life – Dorothy Price (MPAC 7206 – 1963)

Somewhere in France. May 1940

Remembrances

His face still haunts me after all these years, though less so now than before.

The realisation I had killed him, and he had lost the struggle to survive faded in his eyes as I saw him die. The despairing wailing, gurgling groan faded on his lips as death triumphed. I felt his dying breath on my face.

Filled with abhorrence at what I had done, I pulled my bayonet slowly and gently from the dead German's chest. The army had trained us to kill. That was what soldiers did. What the army had not done was to prepare me for what killing another human being did to you.

The blonde, blue-eyed man, who died by my hand, was about my age, perhaps a little older. It was his misfortune to have come my way. His three-man scouting party had walked straight into our quickly prepared ambush. Now they were all dead, done to death without a shot fired or noise made.

"Come on, Manley. Don't dawdle, lad, or we'll have the whole German army down on our necks!" Barked Corporal Thornton. "Let's get out of here on the double. We don't want to end up like Jerry here. And that's what'll happen if their mates find us."

The dead soldier's blood had spurted on my tunic. The bloodstains would turn my khaki into an ugly mud colour when they dried. I tried not to look at the dead man's face with his staring despairing blue eyes, his mouth open in painful terrified shock. They say fear is a reaction, while courage is a decision. There was no courage on my part. The German had been done to death instinctively by my fear of death. Either he died, or I did. I had no choice. I wanted to live.

"Better wipe your mush mate," Smithy muttered, matter-of-factly as he brushed past me, "you've got Fritz's blood splattered all over it."

What happened next is a confusion of half-remembered memories. How we re-joined our platoon, the retreat from pursuing German troops over the following days, remains a blur. The man I had murdered filled my mind for

8

days and weeks afterwards. His death left me with a heavy, sickening feeling. Killing someone is nothing like they show in the films.

Later, questions began to torment me. Had the dead German been married? Did he have children? How would his wife take the news of his death? How would his parents react? More questions would continue to surface. They churned in my brain, around and around and around. How would his mother feel? How would his friends react...? And the questions never seemed to stop.

In 1939 war was coming, and like most young blokes, I wanted to do my bit. I'd signed up with the Territorials first. Nothing the old guys told us about the last war sank in. We wanted to be heroes. We wanted excitement, foreign travel, and adventure. What we got was more than we bargained for and nothing like we imagined. Before I knew it, I found myself enlisted as a full-timer with the KOYLI, the King's Own Yorkshire Light Infantry. That's how I came to serve in the 2nd Battalion.

Proudly wearing my uniform on leave, I'd strutted around Halifax looking for girls to admire me. No luck there, no matter how hard I tried. The army soon shipped us over The Channel to France for our foreign holiday. We were all of us full of it. Young, ignorant, would-be warriors always are. The regiment was off to war again, and we were going to show Jerry a thing or two.

We didn't see any action at first as we wintered in Lille. They called it the Phony war, but it didn't stay phony long. All I can remember of the time before the fighting broke out was endlessly feeling cold. It was a harsh freezing winter. I got to know a local girl, Reine Fournier, and her family. They helped to improve my schoolboy French.

When the fighting started, our battalion seemed to be in constant retreat. We fought a delaying action at the Seine as the bulk of the BEF retreated to Dunkirk. Talk about feeling abandoned at the time as we learned of the evacuation. The so-called Dunkirk miracle was no miracle for those of us left stranded in France. Clashes with the enemy were sporadic. Eventually, we found ourselves being pulled back to Cherbourg.

Did I kill any more Germans? Perhaps. I shot at a few. At sixty or seventy yards, I may only have wounded them, assuming I even hit them. If I'm honest, I don't know, and I prefer not to know. The man I killed still continued to haunt my memories. His dying face continued to fill my nightmares, refusing to leave me alone.

My return to England came courtesy of an exploding artillery shell. The remnant of our battalion was in retreat heading towards the Cherbourg peninsula when it happened.

Smithy was singing a George Formby ditty *Imagine Me On The Maginot Line*, when the shell exploded. He'd just sung the line about clinging to his old tin hat when a piece of the shrapnel went straight through his. He was dead before he fell to the ground. One second alive, the next gone. He copped it while I survived. At least it was quick, and he probably never knew what happened, instant lights out. I lived with nothing worse than a nasty flesh wound. It would leave me with a permanent scar over my left shoulder and arm. Fortunately, it didn't cause any nerve damage. I'd be a liar if I said the wound didn't hurt. It hurt like hell, but at least it wasn't fatal. It got me evacuated back across the Channel from Cherbourg as one of the wounded.

The remnants of the King's Own Yorkshire Light Infantry 2nd/4th Battalion followed, making it back home from Cherbourg. Those who didn't were either dead or in POW camps. I was one of the lucky evacuees.

Back in Blighty, I needed surgery to remove all the remaining bits of shrapnel. My recovery was slow. The wound took a long time to heal completely. Strange what I remember about Smithy. He was always smiling, singing, or whistling a tune. So full of life and living. The nineteen-year-old from Todmorden didn't deserve to die. Nobody deserves to go the way he did. Smithy became another memory writ deep, forever indelibly imprinted in my head.

They let me recover from my wounds long enough before returning me to frontline duty again. By then, they'd made me a corporal and Bill Thornton a Sergeant. North Africa became our next holiday destination as we found ourselves chasing the Jerries out of Tunisia.

The French I picked up back in 1940 proved handy as many locals spoke a version of it. Then it was Salerno and Italy for the remainder of the war. They put our battalion in the vanguard of the action. At the time, all I could remember thinking was the top brass was determined to see us all killed. Somehow, I got through it without a scratch, though plenty of others didn't.

Death in war is horrific. Let no one tell you otherwise. Seeing the remains of those killed in action scars the mind in ways no civilian could ever conceive. The sight of scattered entrails and body parts and the smell of blood leave no room for heroic feelings. Each day in battle is about survival. You never get over the deaths, more so when it's the innocent. The sight of a little girl, her body torn in half, lying next to the remains of her mother aren't sights you forget. No wonder soldiers never talked about these atrocities on returning home. What good would it do? Better to spare your family the grim reality. Bottling all those horrifying sights only results in living with your nightmares. If that's what the mangled bodies of strangers do, then the deaths of the blokes you served alongside are worse.

You remember their faces, smiling, joking, swearing, and complaining. Then you see them killed in an instant without warning. Or you watch them dying in agonising pain. How do you live with that? When you know all about their lives and their families back home? Yet, you continue to live when they don't. What choice do you have? No choice. You are glad to be still alive because your life remains more precious than you could ever have imagined. In war, you're relieved you've survived to breathe another day. You're happy to awake to another sunrise, but you always keep wondering why chance spared you and not the other bloke.

Was I lucky to survive? Or was I fated to live through the horrors of warfare for a reason? I still wonder, and more so when I think about the fate yet to befall me.

My wartime memories stayed imprinted in my brain and would not leave me alone. VE and VJ day came and went, but the nightmare memories continued to plague me, refusing to fade away. It took me a while to readjust to civilian life. My parents were ecstatic to have me back, utterly delighted I had survived when the sons of so many others locally had not. My younger brother also came home safely. The sea had not claimed him. Andrew had managed to stay alive on the ocean waves serving in the navy on Motor Torpedo Boats.

Back in Halifax, I learned from him that his skipper had been a Scotsman by the name of MacKinnon. MacKinnon, he told me, had also come to live in the town and now worked in one of the banks as a junior manager. At the time, I gave him no thought. Years later, it proved to be far more than yet another coincidence. Nothing could possibly be so coincidental. Many more coincidences would follow in the years to come.

To adjust to something like everyday life took me a while. Barely out of the local grammar school when the war began, there had been no time to decide on a career before going off soldiering at eighteen. On returning, I took various temporary jobs, searching for something better to do for a living. I struggled to settle in a job.

A year and a half later, I had met and married Ivy Sharples. Why I did so, I never understood, and I still don't.

11

There were moments when I had considered returning to France to see if I could find Reine Fournier. Thinking back now, I don't know why I didn't. Once back in Halifax, France seemed a faraway place. I experienced a sense of relief to be back in a familiar place. I reasoned Reine may have married someone by now and forgotten me. We scarcely knew one another though her memory remained vivid. Yet, our meeting would lead to another coincidence in future years. One day I would meet her little brother, Henri, again. Not as he had known me during the war as the young British soldier, but as Alice.

Anyway, home was home, and I had my family to think about instead of gallivanting off to foreign parts again. Maybe knowing this turned my thoughts to settling down. Maybe, this also prompted me to believe finding a wife was the answer to all my problems. Did I hope marriage would enable me to live an ordinary life and put the past behind me? I believe it did.

In the beginning, I suppose, it was the physical attraction. Ivy was good-looking in a buxom come-hither kind of way. Not plain, but no great beauty either. During the war, she had served in the Land Army to do her bit. Now, back in in Civvy Street, she was on the hunt for a husband.

We came across one another at a local dance. Ivy was outgoing. A real tease who loved to flirt. At first, she showed no genuine romantic interest in me. She chose to ignore all my advances. After a while, I gave up attempting to get together with her. Ivy must have felt thwarted because I was no longer falling for her flirting and teasing charms. Either that or the bloke she fancied showed no interest. To this day, I believe Ivy had her set her cap on Eddie Baker, a local lad I had known in my youth. When he went off with another young woman, Ivy changed her mind about me. I often think these days I was her second-best choice. Still, when we did get together, we had our moments. Our romance, once it began, was more lust than love. If I'm honest, lust brought the two of us together. We both yearned for sex.

I was a quiet chap before the war and even quieter in many ways after returning. Ivy was vivacious and full of life. She was keen to land herself a husband, as were most young women back in those days. She hooked me without too much hard work. Phil Manley proved an easy catch.

Marry in haste and repent at leisure is a saying worth noting, but I've also seen cases of marrying at leisure and repenting in haste. Either way, the best matches do not always turn out for the best. Let me add, as a married couple, we rubbed along and made the best of our lives. I think we both probably wondered if we could have done better with someone else.

12

Ivy was one of those women we call brussen in Yorkshire. Brussen was a local expression for someone loudmouthed who liked to think they were somehow special. Brussen came from brazen, or brassy, with its undertone of shameless impudence. Not too bad a description of Ivy as she grew older. The longer we were married, the worse she became, and the more unbearable.

It took a while for Ivy to get pregnant. When she did, she was resentful throughout the pregnancy. Although, having now experienced pregnancy, I probably have greater sympathy with her experiences. Once Cathy was born in 1949, Ivy surprisingly took to her new maternal role. By then, our once physically passionate romance had already fizzled out into disappointing oblivion.

Having a child for Ivy became more about conforming to expectations. Our marriage drifted into a loveless state without even knowing how or why. It took time for the two of us to understand our relationship was anything but love and roses. Whatever feelings we had for one another became more of a routine played out daily. We stuck it out because it was the done thing. Staying wed was expected by our families, friends, and relatives. Marriage meant for better or worse for most people. Divorce was not considered respectable. It was also expensive and needed one of us to commit adultery. Neither of us was inclined to be the guilty party or to get co-respondents. Besides, I loved my daughter, so I stayed.

Cathy was my girl in every way. Not only in her looks but also in her quiet manner. I couldn't find it in myself to abandon Cathy's upbringing to her mother's clutches. The blame could not rest with Ivy alone. Returning to an ordinary life could not silence nor stop the horrors. They kept resurfacing in my head from time to time, in fact, too often. The nightmares returned to plague my days and nights long after returning to Civvy Street. Though intermittent, they came and went, haunting my sleep and sometimes surfacing in the day when least wanted. Witnessing death and destruction was not easily driven from my mind.

There were spells when my life became so seriously blighted by the memories, I thought I would go completely crazy. Everyone expected men like me to cope. Some coped, and some didn't. I didn't. At least not as well as I ought to have done. Some experiences you can never erase, not even with time. Mine kept on returning. Back then, the medical world had acknowledged conditions like mine as genuine psychological illnesses. Many of us were too proud to admit to suffering from such conditions. To admit to such a thing was still seen as unmanly, even cowardly by some. A few ex-soldiers, I heard, had committed suicide when they were unable to cope any longer. I pretended to confront my demons and gave the impression of doing so. Something needed to happen to change my life.

I had taken several jobs but found no satisfaction in any of them. The longest one I held down was at the local biscuit factory. My mathematical skills got me work as a wages clerk at MacVitie's. The job lacked challenge and proved boring in the extreme. I desperately needed a change from the boredom and monotony. The work had soon become slavish wage drudgery. There was a desperate need for teachers to fill the gaps wreaked by the war. The pay was better than my current job, so I applied. As an ex-soldier with Higher School qualifications, I found myself accepted. At least I got away from Ivy for a short time while I underwent teacher training.

Training?

What a joke training turned out. I spent quite a few hours practicing copperplate handwriting with chalk on blackboards until my tutor was satisfied. I wrote a few essays, and bingo, suddenly it was over. I passed the final exams, which were not exactly demanding, and qualified. There was no problem finding a job. The local authority could not hire enough emergency trained teachers quickly enough. Ivy was delighted as more money came into the household once I started in a local Junior school. Before long, she had pressured me into buying a bigger house in a better area with better furniture. Not that I could blame her for wanting something better

So, we moved to a bigger, modern house, but it did nothing to improve either her nature or our relationship. We co-existed. Her looks hardened even more, and the once passably attractive buxom appearance spoiled. It is easy to suppose her constant hectoring drove me to drink. It did not. I could not seem to adjust to the life I was living. It didn't surprise me how many ex-servicemen like me had taken to drinking. Another bad habit I acquired during the war was smoking. Once hooked, I became a heavy chain smoker addicted to the demon nicotine.

Like so many youngsters, I'd started on Woodbines or coffin nails, as we jokingly called them. Cheap and nasty they led me to switch to Capstan full-strength. Capstan full strength was a real man's smoke. It didn't take long before the wheezing, coughing and breathlessness took a hold of my lungs. Even a switch to filtered brands, in the mistaken belief these were healthier, did nothing to improve my breathing and coughing. I should have known better. Smoking two packs of twenty cigarettes a day didn't help.

A couple of ex-soldiers who worked in the same school got me in the habit of lunchtime pub sessions. A pint of Tetley's bitter soon became two, then three. Then it became a regular habit to go down to the pub on an evening.

Teaching had its moments, but a class full of forty smelly eleven years could be wearing. Trying to get the best of these boys to pass the grammar school tests proved demanding. A few made it, but not through a lack of effort.

Materially life improved for us as post-war austerity ended. Old Mac was right. As a nation, we had never had it as good.

The TV set I purchased in 1957 kept Ivy happy as I whiled away the evenings keeping pints of Ramsden's bitter company. Returning home in a cosy beer haze became an all too frequent occurrence. Her verbal lashings only sounded comical in my drunken stupors. More often, I ended up sleeping on the settee downstairs. The more the drinking took hold, the more our life drifted messily apart. Heavy drinking, to drown out the torture of past horrors exacted its toll. Too many bouts of drunkenness, heavy smoking, and poor eating habits had inevitable consequences. They contributed to my early demise. No one else was to blame. It was all my own doing, all my fault. This is why I reckon I ended up dead ahead of time and missed my own funeral.

Chapter 3

Can't Get Used To Losing You – Andy Williams (CBS AAG 138 – 1963)

Saturday 24 September 1966

"Is this one of your school friends?" Ivy asked Cathy politely, giving me a pleasant smile.

Cathy, taken aback, seemed unsure what to say. Almost stammering, she introduced me. "M-Mum, this is A-Alice. She came around to see how I was getting on."

"So good of you to come visiting. Cathy has always been a quiet girl, one without many friends. Have you known each other long?"

"Yes," I began, then realised I needed to be cautious, "we were in different classes, but since then, we've gotten to know each other better."

"That's nice. Cathy has taken the death of her father badly, haven't you, dear?" Cathy nodded, giving me a peculiar look, vaguely suggesting a half-smile.

"It was a terrible shock," sighed Ivy, "he was a good man at heart even though he didn't always show it. We both miss him, don't we, Cathy?"

Cathy nodded.

"My Mum's a widow, too," I responded with a half-truth.

"Oh, dear. When did your father die, dear?" Ivy laid on her sympathetic voice, the one she was so expert at doing.

I didn't know, so I gave her a vague answer. "It was a few years ago."

"So, are you the only one?"

"I have a sister who's thirteen and an older brother who's just turned eighteen."

"What are they called?" Ivy's interest wasn't just out of politeness. It was her typical insidious way of learning everyone's business. Except, somehow, it didn't seem to be at all insidious, and strangely sympathetic.

"Edie is my sister. Edie's short for Edith after my Gran. Frank's my brother."

"Do I know your mother by any chance?"

I knew for a fact there was precious little chance they knew one another. So, I pressed on, doing my best to give the impression she might. "She's called Lorna. Her maiden name was Reeve. Do you know her?"

Ivy shook her head. "Can't say I do. Cathy, why haven't you made your friend a cup of tea? You will stay for one, won't you, Alice? I could certainly do with one. Can you put this shopping away for me and brew a pot for us, love? There are some ginger biscuits in the tin. That walk to the shops has tired me out."

The bumptious and loud-mouthed Ivy I knew had changed in such a short time since my demise.

Cathy was understandably reluctant to leave me alone with Ivy. I saw it in her eyes. Was she afraid I might say something to give myself away? There was no chance of that happening. At this moment, the realisation struck me forcibly as to who I had become. I could never be Phil Manley again. Like it or not, I was stuck being Alice.

"I miss my husband," Ivy confessed in a whisper. "It happened so suddenly. I never had the chance to tell him how I felt about him. Cathy took his death badly. She was a real Daddy's girl. His passing has hit her hard, and life without him is so very different. I miss the sound of him coming home from school. He was a teacher, you know."

Her eyes welled up in genuine sadness. What a shame she never told me how she felt when I was alive.

"Phil was his name," she continued with an unexpected sadness. "He never got over his experiences in the war. He used to have shocking nightmares. Many a time, he would wake up in the night, sweating, sometimes screaming, and rambling on about the terrible things he had witnessed. Very disturbing they were, horrible to say the least."

She stopped speaking, momentarily lost in reverie, then she let out a series of sighs sounding like sobs. "Poor sod. It must have been terrible."

It was.

I could hear the kettle whistling and the clinking of cups in the kitchen. Tears welled in Ivy's eyes. I wanted to put my arms around her. We had, after all, shared a life together for more than twenty years. Resisting the urge, I restrained myself. Whatever I was, I was no longer her husband. Our marriage vows had stipulated until death do us part. Death had parted me from my body. It was six feet under, and technically I was dead and buried. There was no guarantee I would remain alive in Alice's body. For all, I knew she might return, and I might be forced to leave. Yet here I was, watching my wife, or ex-wife, depending upon a point of view, ready to cry. Reassurance felt necessary.

"I know what you mean," I sighed, ready to tell a whopper, "I wish I'd had one last hug from my dad."

"I suppose, it does no good to dwell on these things. What was is no longer. Losing someone is never easy. We have to carry on, no matter how hard it is." The tender moments had passed.

I nodded as if to agree. Was it an act? The thought was unavoidable. Ivy could lay it on thick, as I knew from experience. Something told me this was a show of genuine emotion. Hardly surprising, the more I pondered on it. You live with someone long enough, and you know by instinct when the truth comes out.

"Cathy needs a good friend." Ivy continued.

"I'll be a very good friend to her."

Then the conversation changed as she inspected me closely. I had lost all dress sense, according to my surrogate sister Edie. My hair was tied in a messy ponytail. As for putting on makeup, I hadn't a clue. Cathy was going to have to teach me how. Adapting to being a young female was going to be some undertaking. One I had already dreaded.

"Alice, a young woman of your age, should not still be wearing knee socks," Ivy commented on my appearance. "You should be wearing stockings or these new-fangled tights. I know you're quite tall. Do you have a problem finding the right size?"

Bizarrely I found myself blushing. The simple fact of it was I had not mastered the skill of wearing stockings. I was struggling with remembering to put a bra on each morning. Most days, I forgot. The fact my breasts were tiny didn't help. They were smaller than my male breasts had been when I was alive. Lorna, my surrogate mother, would gently remind me to go and put my bra on, although honestly, it seemed pointless. The mention of nylons made me blush.

The whole suspender belt thing was another item I was struggling with in my new identity. At least I was spared wearing a roll on because I was so slim. Edie was of little use or help. In all honesty, I was too embarrassed to ask her. It just did not feel right asking a young girl for advice. Lorna struggled to communicate with me at first as I did with her. There was a difficulty in the way for me. It did not help that what remained of the man in me found Lorna an attractive woman. Now I was female, and her flesh and blood, it made it even more awkward. My response to Ivy's comment was polite.

18

"It's the cost," I replied. "I have some nylon stockings, but I need to look after them, so I don't wear them all the time. My Mum's widow pension and child allowance doesn't stretch to many luxuries."

That was true.

The Liddell household was not affluent. The life insurance had paid off the mortgage with a small sum left over, but that was all. Since the death of her husband, Lorna Liddell found it hard to keep us dressed and fed. She was no longer a housewife but a working woman down at the biscuit factory. The same biscuit factory where I had once worked.

Edie was trying to get a paper round to earn herself some pocket money. I would need money too and would have to find a Saturday job. Lorna and Frank insisted on me staying on at school to sit my GCE A Levels. I could have a Saturday job, but on no account was I to think about leaving school. They said I was too bright and would get a better job if I passed my exams; maybe I might even get to university. Somehow the family would manage.

Frank willingly tipped up his apprentice wage to Lorna to help. He was a lovely young chap. The kind of young man I would not have minded for a son. Instead, I had Frank for a brother.

Chapter 4

Why Can't A Woman Be More Like A Man? – Rex Harrison
My Fair Lady (Original Soundtrack Recording
(CBS SBRG 72237 LP 1964)

Saturday, 1 October 1966.

Cathy was busy applying whatever it was to my face. She stopped and passed the hand mirror to me. "Take a look. Do you think you look more attractive now?"

The mirror did not lie. I could not deny the improvement. The skilful art of cosmetic concealment had banished my few skin blemishes. There was more colour in my cheeks. My eyes looked enlarged and more attractive. The bags under my eyes had almost vanished. She had done a great job hiding my spots. I nodded. "You're right. It does make me look more attractive. But I don't know if I can manage to do it myself."

"I'm going to teach you how. So, let's take it all off, and you can have a go. It's not half as hard as you think it is. You don't see many young women going without makeup."

Edie was looking on. Cathy let nothing slip and made sure our conversation remained guarded.

"Alice used to do her own before she lost her memory. She could make herself look gorgeous and well-groomed." Edie commented.

"She will again, won't you, Alice?" Cathy muttered as she helped me wipe the makeup off.

"You still haven't answered me. Yes, I know it makes me look more attractive. Is it just for me? Or is it only to attract men and boys? If that's the case, I'm not interested."

Cathy finished and sighed. "It makes me feel good looking at a more pleasing version of myself. It's like a mask. I don't do it just for the boys. But it makes me feel good knowing boys are looking and finding me attractive, I won't deny it."

"So, it makes you feel more confident about yourself?"

"Yes, I suppose it does. I do feel more confident if my makeup makes me look good."

One of the things I was starting to learn was how insecure the female sex could be. Not just about their appearance, but in general about lots of other things. A woman's looks were all-important. As a man, I had never given it much thought. Yes, I had to be clean-shaven. Yes, a visit to the barbers to get my hair cut was a fortnightly habit. Habits learned in the army had never left me.

In a female body, it was proving altogether different. I was already beginning to share some of the female anxieties about my looks, no doubt encouraged by Edie and Cathy. As a man, when I had looked at my face in the mirror, it was a cursory activity. A quick checklist to ensure I had shaved sufficiently close and had combed my hair. As a female, the mirror became an addictive implement, an essential tool for viewing my face more than several times a day. I lied to myself, saying it was to accustom myself to my new state of being. The truth was I was experiencing a curious tinge of vanity.

"Now, what do we do first?" Cathy prompted, placing the array of cosmetics in front of me.

"Make sure my face is clean before I put anything on?"

"Good. It's clean. Now, start. Step by step. What's first?"

"Moisturiser?"

"Yes. Because you've got slightly greasy skin, go easy on my moisturiser. It's for dry skin. We'll have to find one which suits you. Also, we could do with a more suitable foundation for your paler skin tone."

I'd never appreciated the artistry involved. Matching skin tones, eye colour, and all the rest was overwhelming. It took me ages to get the simple things right. The eyes were worse. I'd never liked fiddling with my eyes, but Cathy insisted eye makeup was the key to getting *the look*. She was making me put on the young and cool trendy pale makeup worn by the fashion models. When she suggested I spit on the mascara before trying to apply it, I was disgusted. I ended up getting a little water, repelled by the unhygienic suggestion. Funnily enough, I never gave it a second thought later on.

When it came to lipstick, both Cathy and Edie fell about laughing. I had asked why I shouldn't wear bright red lipstick.

"That's for old women like your…" she almost said wife.

"Mum," I interjected before she could say anything further.

"Yeah. Pale lipsticks are fab, like Cathy's *Pink Meringue*. That's what you should try. They look cool," Edie stated confidently. "Go on then. Try it."

The lipstick was by Max Factor. "Is it expensive?" I asked.

Cathy smiled at me. "Not so expensive. My mum gave me some pocket money to buy it." From her face, I knew Cathy had no intention of telling the truth.

My long hair had become a nightmare, stretching down my back for a good eight inches. No matter how hard I tried to master the intricacies of different buns, I couldn't manage to do them. They looked a mess. It was either a ponytail or a ponytail. I couldn't expect Edie to help me out every morning. The only solution would be to have it cut short.

"Do you think I'd suit one of those Sassoon bob hairstyles? Nice and Short? Should I get one of these? What do you think?"

"Definitely." Cathy's answer was quite emphatic. "You'd look cool."

Even Edie signalled immediate approval. "It would suit you. A bob cut would work brilliantly with the shape of your face but without a fringe and falling just below your ears. Besides, you have such a thick thatch a straight bob would look the biz. Cropping it too short, and you'd look a mess. What you need to do is to brush it more thoroughly and more often, like every day. That's something you haven't done since you came home from the hospital. By the way, you have a lot of split ends. You need to deal with them, 'cos your hair's a mess."

"Split ends?" I queried, displaying my cluelessness. The explanation made me feel a little wiser.

There were so many questions about being a female I needed answers to and fast.

A song from the film *My Fair Lady* kept playing in my head for the rest of the day. *Why can't a woman be more like a man?* Adapting to being a female was going to be no easy matter.

I had been out of the hospital for two weeks. There was talk of me going back to the Grammar school to complete my A-Levels. It was the last thing I wanted. I was seventeen and would soon be eighteen. I could have left school already. Lorna had insisted that her Alice stayed on in the Sixth Form. From all the information I had gathered from Edie and Frank, Alice had been a bright spark. The teachers expected her to pass all three exams with top grades at A-Level. There was a strong possibility that she would get a university place.

Going back to school had me worried. How the hell was I going to pass these A-Levels? The idea of getting behind a school desk again was a worrying prospect. More so as I thought about being thrust among a class full of teenage girls. It was true I had had to write essays while undertaking the emergency teacher-training course, but that had been quite a while ago. And yes, years ago, I had passed the then equivalents of A-Levels back in the day of the Higher Certificates. Doing the same now years later was going to be something of a challenge.

Then I thought, how hard could it be going into a classroom again as a pupil? I had taken part in ferocious, bloody battles during the war. I had seen men die in horrific ways. Surely, coping in a class full of girls would be easy? No, it would not be easy, but it might be the only way I could educate myself to live like a woman. I still had a lot to learn. Then the thought struck me. I was young again and had a lifetime ahead, which struck me forcibly. It meant I would need to work for a living.

Chapter 5

Good Morning Little Schoolgirl – The Yardbirds
(Columbia DB7391 – 1964)

Monday, 3 October 1966

The school was concerned about allowing me to return. After all, I'd lost my memory, so presumably, I didn't remember anything they had taught me. Even my handwriting differed from Alice's, an obvious giveaway.

Teacher training had ensured my handwriting was almost calligraphic and fit for blackboard use. Alice's original handwriting was typical of a teenage girl. Her trademark use of heart shapes instead of dots on i's must have annoyed her teachers. Her script was large and expansive, left sloping, eight to nine words to a line. Mine was compact, right sloping copperplate italic. I could squeeze ten to eleven words on a line of foolscap. Then there was my clipped manner of speaking.

According to Lorna, Edie, and Frank, how I *now* spoke was also different. The use of slang words such as *cool, fab, choice,* and *dig* had vanished from new Alice's vocabulary. They found my adult-sounding diction strange. There was no way I could act like Alice of old. For a start, I had no idea what she had been like, though this was not strictly true. I'd overheard my new family talking about me in muted tones. Their Alice had been a dreamer, a quiet indecisive girl prone to giggling and easily bullied. I, the *new* Alice, was a contradicting opposite. Serious, strangely withdrawn, with fewer smiles, careless about my appearance. As the replacement Alice, this summoned me up. I would have to change. I was no longer a disillusioned middle-aged man, and I had no reason to behave like one.

The idea of returning to school filled me with dread. This was the last thing I wanted to do. After some thought, I concluded I had no choice but to go. Like it or not, I had another lifetime of work ahead. Gaining some certificates would help me choose what I did in the future. So, on Monday morning, I donned her school uniform of a navy-blue skirt, green shirt, striped tie, and uniform jacket. Edie watched in amazement as I tied a perfect Windsor knot in front of the mirror.

24

"When did you learn to do that?" Her face had frozen in astonishment. "You could never tie a knot properly, let alone one so neat. Frank has always had to do them for us. And it's never been as a neat."

It was yet another giveaway, and one that had never even occurred to me. As a girl, would I even know how to tie a Windsor knot? Probably not.

"I've taught myself how to do it properly, it wasn't hard," I muttered confidently.

Edie didn't question my reply, thankfully accepting my explanation.

"You'll have to show me how. You do it so much better than Frank."

"I'll show you how later." I let out an enormous sigh. "I suppose we had better set off."

On went the school raincoat and school hat. I made a final check of my satchel's contents and readied myself for the bizarre prospect of returning behind a school desk. This time as a pupil in an all-girls school.

An over-anxious Lorna accompanied us on this first day back.

The school was near to home, a short walk away. I had often passed it in my previous life and was no stranger to the place. Of the inside of the building, with its corridors and classrooms, I knew nothing. This would prove a serious trial. I would have to become a quick learner to find my way around the building.

Although we arrived early, the school was already filling with pupils. Almost straight away, I noticed peculiar looks from a group of girls about my age, including a red-haired, red-faced chubby girl. If I was supposed to know them, I didn't, but it was clear they knew me.

After a short conversation with my mother to confirm my amnesiac condition, the headmistress summoned a girl into her office. Jackie Booth was in my registration group and, according to my teachers, one of my friends.

As soon as I saw her, I felt sorry for Jackie. I could tell she seemed pleased to see me. Yet she seemed unhappy at the same time. I had seen the same look before as a teacher. The kids may have been ten and eleven, and they may have been boys, but the glances were the same. Poor Jackie was all I could think as I worked her out.

Bony and tiny, barely five feet tall, Jackie had wavy mousy hair. The lenses of her butterfly-style spectacles made her eyes appear larger than usual which suggested she was short-sighted. The poor mite's chin appeared ravaged by teen acne. Instantly I had complete sympathy for her. At five foot seven or eight, I towered over her. Skinny and awkward, I might be, but at least my complexion was clear. We were about to become a peculiar sight. Again. The headmistress reminded Jackie of their previous conversation, presumably about me. Then I was back into school life as a Sixth Former.

My schoolboy days were long gone. Memories of those days had by now become distant. Yet what was happening to me was so intensely sharp, focussed, and at the same time unreal. Here I was, sitting in a class full of teenage girls. A deceased middle-aged man in a young woman's body. Nothing could be more bizarre, and I defy anyone to tell me otherwise. Somehow, I had to rationalise this craziness. Placed in this strange situation I had to adapt to survive or end up mad as a hatter. From here on in it would be about getting my life together as a schoolgirl.

Identifying the ones who planned on giving me grief didn't take long. Bullies are found everywhere, in all walks and at all stages of life. The ones here would be in for a surprise. In my new guise, they would not find me a pushover.

The first lesson behind a school desk was French. It was an O Level re-sit group of eight girls. I had glanced through Alice's old exercise notebooks and her most recent work. She seemed to have been quite good going by the marks and praising comments. What a pity she had missed getting a re-sit pass three times in a row. French had been her Achilles heel in an otherwise academically high achieving record. Maybe I could rectify this one failure.

Stationed on the outskirts of Lille in 1940, I had made the acquaintance of a local family. A little more accurately, I had taken a fancy to their eldest daughter. Reine Fournier was seventeen. She spoke no English, and I spoke only a smattering of schoolboy French, rather badly. Nothing ever happened between us. Her ten-year-old brother Henri proved a trial making sure our love life never got underway. I did, however, become very friendly with her family visiting them whenever there was an opportunity. During the winter, I made a serious attempt to improve my French with the Fournier's help. The colloquial French I picked up became useful when I later found myself serving in Tunisia.

I suspected the teacher would want to check my knowledge, which was why he bombarded me with questions almost immediately.

The man struck me as insufferable and snooty. His accent sounded affected, but then I was no expert. It was likely he was yet another middle-aged ex-officer finding employment as a post-war teacher.

"Comment tu t'appeles, madamoiselle?"

"Je suis Alice...Liddell, monsieur."

26

"Comment allez-vous?"

"Bien, merci."

Then he decided to get clever. *"Quelle est votre compréhension du français parlé, mademoiselle Alice? Est-ce pauvre, adéquat ou excellent?"*

I responded in my most polite manner. *"Je suis désolé, monsieur. Je ne suis pas qualifié pour le dire. Vous, en tant que professeur, êtes la meilleure personne à décider."*

"Bien répondu jeune demoiselle. Quite right, too, I am the teacher and best qualified to say. *Impressionnant.* It seems your illness has not affected your linguistic skills. I shall check your written grammar later."

A promise he would keep, which I doubted would go so well. Though I had picked up spoken French to a tolerable, if not fluent level, the written side was another matter. Perhaps, I should have been a little less clever. Some of the girls in the class gave me decidedly unpleasant looks. There would be a price to pay for my cleverness if I wasn't careful.

Alice had passed seven GCE O levels the year before entering the Lower Sixth, unfortunately not French. She still needed a pass at O level, having failed the November and summer re-sits. That would need rectifying when the time came to re-sit the exam. I would make sure I passed, as it seemed a foreign language was one of the requirements to obtain a university place.

General Studies came next. Twenty-five or so girls made up my group. When they looked in my direction, their stares made me feel self-conscious, exposed, and vulnerable. I couldn't help wondering if they could see straight through me to the man masquerading inside. What a stupid thought, I reassured myself. There was absolutely no possibility it could happen. For all I knew, the sight of me, a dead pupil, resurrected and sitting in the same classroom could be freaking them out. To them, I might be one of the living dead. Maybe, I was. I had died, and I was alive again. It was utter nonsense when I thought it through logically. For most of the entire lesson, I sat rigidly worrying what they might be thinking about me.

The teacher handed out quotes to consider and discuss in groups. Mine received one by Giorgio Vasari, some Renaissance writer on art and artists.

"Men of genius sometimes accomplish most when they work the least, for they are thinking out inventions and forming in their minds the perfect idea that they subsequently express with their hands."

My decision to remain silent proved sensible. For the briefest moment, I toyed with saying something. Then I thought better of it as I almost blurted out, was it only men who had the ideas? Didn't women enter into the discussion? Fortunately, another girl picked up the objection. What a relief!

The history class came next. This was a popular subject, given the size of the group. Twenty girls, including myself, filled the room. The teacher didn't press me during the lesson, which was a relief. I still hadn't read up on all of Alice's notes. Pleasant and enthusiastic the teacher had a passion for the subject. You could see this by the way the group responded to her with equal enthusiasm. When the lesson ended, relief surged through me. Thankfully, it was the last session of the day. Mentally drained and physically exhausted, I couldn't wait to get back home, knowing I had survived.

"How did it go?" Edie asked, as we strolled slowly homeward.

"OK, I suppose," I replied with a shrug of the shoulders. "It could have been worse."

"Any problems with Janice Barrowclough and her mates?"

"Who?"

"Redhead. With curly hair? Red in the face? Short? Tubby."

"No. Not yet, although I saw someone fitting that description. I've only just started and can't remember any of the girls or their names. It's all new to me. Like I've never been here before. Who is she anyway? I take it she was no friend of mine."

The look in Edie's eyes spoke a library.

"So, she's the one to watch out for? What do I need to know about her?"

"Some days, you would come home in tears. Barrowclough was horrible to you and Jackie Booth. She got some of her so-called friends to gang up on you both. They called you horrible names, said all sorts of nasty, unpleasant things too. It was what they said. It upset you both. There weren't many days when you didn't come home hurt and upset. I was hoping Mum would have let you leave school after what happened in the hospital. You ought to have left the place when your friend Angie Thornton did at the end of the Fifth Form.

"Angie Thornton?"

"She was your best friend right from infants until she left. Angie didn't let anyone bully her or you. You used to tell me how she stood up to bullies. What a shame you can't remember her. I liked Angie a lot." Edie smiled, remembering something.

"What?"

"Sweets. Angie always had some sweets she shared with you. She always gave me one too. I liked her. She was lovely."

28

"I wonder what happened to her?"

Who had been this mysterious friend and protector? Bored with reading Alice's history notes and essays, I welcomed Edie's distraction.

"Angie works in a chemist's shop in the town centre. For a short while, Angie used to come visiting after she left school. Once she started working, she didn't have the time. I suppose having a boyfriend didn't help. I remember she told you she spent a lot of time with him in the evenings." Edie paused sufficiently long enough to get a breath before continuing. "I ran into her on Saturday afternoon when she'd just finished work. She was waiting to catch a bus and looked so cool and stylish. Gone all Mod now. You should see how she dresses. And her hairstyle! It's so fab. Cut short with one side longer than the other, in one of those Mod hairstyles."

Angie's taste in fashion clearly impressed Edie.

My curiosity, I had to admit, was aroused. I suppose something prompted me to want to know more. The more I learned, the better I'd be equipped to deal with life as Alice.

"So, did she ask after me?"

"Of course, she did. I think Angie was shocked when I told her what had happened to you. Do you know, she wanted to come round to see you straight away but...?"

"But what?"

"But I told her to wait a while. I explained how you'd lost your memory and didn't even know who we were, let alone anyone else. Mum had said it could be quite some time before you got your memory back. I told Angie it might not be a good idea until you did. I said I'd let her know."

"So, you haven't spoken to her since?"

"No. You've still not got your memory back, have you?" Edie became unexpectedly defensive. "Besides, don't get me wrong. Your new self is nothing like your old self."

"My *new* self? Go on. Explain."

Edie stared at me with unexpected strangeness. It was the same look someone gave when speaking to a stranger. It had kept reappearing, and this after we seemed to have established some kind of sisterly relationship.

"Explain? Explain! That's not like the old you. You would never have said that. You're just so..."

"Different?"

"Yes."

"How?" The time had arrived to force some honesty.

"It's like you are somebody completely different, another person. You're nothing like the Alice I know and grew up with, you're like someone else."

"You try coming around without a single memory, not even knowing your name. You'd be different."

My words made Edie pause. "It's not just what you say. You're nothing like you used to be. You don't talk like you did. You don't even walk the way you did. Everything about you is so different. You're so... mannish. It's like you've become a lad. It's weird. I mean, you forget to wear your bra, you sit with your legs wide apart flashing your knickers. It's as if you've forgotten all the basics of being a girl."

The warning sirens were going off. I needed to try harder.

"Which is why Cathy is helping me. I've forgotten it all."

"And who is she?" Edie's voice filled with suspicion. "You say you met her when you were in the hospital and became friendly? When did this happen? Because I don't remember seeing her there."

"Well, Edie, we did meet there, and we became friendly. We exchanged addresses and said we'd visit each other when I came out. And we have, as you've seen. Maybe I need a stranger to be a friend with whom I can share my problems."

I hoped Cathy would not forget our cover stories.

Chapter 6

Walk - Don't Run '64 – The Ventures (Liberty LIB 96 – 1964)

Thursday, 6 October.

Edie's description of Janice Barrowclough was accurate. When the angels handed out looks to girls at birth, they scraped the barrel bottom for hers. Heaven had been mean, extremely mean. Plain would be a polite description. If there was one thing I could say in my defence, I did at least have a pretty face. I might be tall, and I might have a boyish figure with a tiny bust, but I certainly wasn't ugly, far from it. Whatever bullying Alice had suffered before, I wouldn't tolerate it. I would snuff it out straight away. No teenage harpy would be allowed to take advantage of Jackie or me.

Barrowclough always surrounded herself with at least a couple of like-minded chums willing to assist in the abuse. It wasn't long before it started and became yet another new experience in this girl's life.

Unlike boys bullying, whose pack mentality often escalated into physical abuse, girls bullying girls worked differently. The bullying was more akin to psychological warfare. Cathy had spoken to me at length about the kind of mind games played out between girls and what I might expect. Girls' bullying a girl was an exercise in mental torture aimed at the core of who you were. My first-hand experience arrived soon enough.

In my new guise, I decided not to be a loner. Mixing with other girls would enable me to become accepted and to assimilate into my new gender. This turned out easier to do than I expected.

As a female, I found myself instinctively drawn to other girls for companionship. The pull to belong differed from the ones I had experienced as a boy and a man. Yes, it was about feeling safe and secure, but also about much more. Why this was so, I gradually began to understand. Girls, and women, generally seemed much more dependent on one another than boys and men did.

The sneering, unkind comments Barrowclough made initially took me by surprise. Today, as Jackie and I walked along the corridor to registration, I was prepared. Our misfortune and good fortune lay in belonging to the brainy group. At least it ensured Jackie and I were not in the same room as our tormentors.

Poor Jackie, I had noticed, trembled whenever we passed Barrowclough and her buddies. Her tiny bony knuckles went chalk-white from gripping the satchel straps in anticipation of the insults.

"Leave this to me, Jackie," I spoke with complete confidence. We had experienced insults for the last two days. Barrowclough, I could see, was readying to spit out some more abuse. Her coterie of three friends leaning against a classroom wall began tittering as we approached.

"Look who's coming! Ladder legs and her leprechaun. Hey ladder legs, can you receive TV signals up there?" The other girls made twittering sounds reminiscent of a blue-tits chorus.

I let out a pretend sweet sigh, and battle commenced. "Barrowclough, you always sound better with your mouth shut. When I bother to see your lips moving, all I ever hear is blah, blah, blah."

My words took her by surprise. No one had ever known Alice to respond to her insults. My reply was so unexpected and delivered with such casual panache even I was impressed. Her chums put their hands up to their mouths to try to stop themselves from sniggering. They failed. Barrowclough reddened slightly more than she was already and tried to come up with something to trade as an insult in return.

Fatefully she stuttered. "I-I-I don't remember asking your opinion… Miss Blackpool Tower. Go to hell, Liddell!"

With an evil glint in my eyes, I turned and walked back towards her. What I did next was what I remembered boys doing when they bullied someone. A good head taller gave me an advantage. I loomed over Barrowclough using my height to intimidate her. The darkness in my words aroused a look of fear in her as she heard my words and began to cower in my shade.

"Go to hell? Where do you think I came back from, Barrowclough? Heaven? Wrong. By the way, your tie needs straightening." Taking hold of her school tie, I straightened it, pushing the knot up so hard it tightened harder around her throat.

My unexpected physical intimidation was scarier than even I imagined. Barrowclough kept backing away as I kept closing the gap between us. The wall behind stopped her retreat. In a whisper so only she and Jackie could hear, I added the threat of violence in a most unfeminine way. "I'd slap your little piggy face until it matched your hair. But that would be cruelty to animals, and I wouldn't want a visit from the RSPCA."

Jackie Booth looked stunned and began giggling, delighted by my words

32

and action. As we walked away, she said, "Gosh! You were so funny and so scary at the same time."

"Was I?" I replied, trying to play it down, but I could not stop smirking the more I thought about what I had said and done.

Jackie sniggered, "I've never seen Ginge look like that. For á second or two, I thought she was going to fill her knickers. You scared her witless. Hell's bells, Alice! You've changed."

"You'd better believe it. After you've been declared dead and come back to the world of the living, nothing will ever scare you again. By the time I've done with Barrowclough, she'll avoid coming near us. If anyone else tries it on, they'll have me to deal with, and I won't let anyone push me around ever again."

The skirmish was over but not the war. Barrowclough would wish she had never started the day the way she had.

The morning passed without mishap.

Round two of my encounters with Janice Barrowclough took place as I left the dining room. Surprisingly, I hadn't intimidated her enough. She seemed insistent on a rematch. Surrounded by four girls as if strength in numbers would somehow protect her, she began trading more nastiness.

"You should have died and not bothered coming back." Barrowclough hissed as I walked past her.

"But I'm back now, and I'm planning to give you and your friends some truly nasty and unpleasant times. When I've done with you, and with them," I stared menacingly in their direction, "you'll dread seeing me."

"Huh. I'm not scared of you, beanpole. None of us are."

I gave her another one of those scary stares. "You should be. I haven't started on you and your chums yet. When I do, you'll wish I hadn't."

She looked away, unable to meet my eyes. "We don't like you."

Poor old Janice, resorting to the kind of reply infants make when they don't know what else to say.

"Gosh!" I exclaimed, faking mock surprise. "For a moment, I almost gave a damn. Frankly, Miss Pigsy! I don't care if you don't like me."

My casually delivered insult hit her hard. Before she could respond, I quickly added, "Barrowclough, you remind everyone of a penny. Two-faced and not worth much. It's a shame you can't see yourself as others do. Take a good look at yourself. You'll soon see what an ugly, nasty piece of work you really are. Shoo! Go on, shoo, clear off. I don't need dirt like you under my feet."

The Miss Pigsy comment, and the dismissive off-hand way I delivered it, broke her. Momentarily, I felt sorry for her. Then I reasoned she deserved a dose of her own brand of maliciousness.

When word spread how I'd dealt with Barrowclough, I speedily acquired a reputation for standing no-nonsense. Pigsy, my new nickname for her, had caught on by the end of the day. As a result, I found myself with quite a few new friends by the end of the week. Girls flocked to a safety net I suddenly appeared to provide.

The first encounter with Barrowclough was mine, but not the war. There would be other skirmishes. For now, I was dealing with a broken enemy in retreat.

The boys from our adjacent school were a different matter.

In my past life, I had attended The Heath Grammar School, an all-boys institution with its origins dating back to the Tudors. Now I was a pupil at the girl's half of Crossley & Porter Grammar.

Our two school halves formed the school established by the Crossley brothers in the 1850s. The Crossley's parents had founded the carpet mill in Dean Clough. They had amassed a fortune as demand had grown for carpets. Their two sons used some of the inheritance to become charitable benefactors and established the school. Years ago, the school had taken in boarders, but boarding had ceased a long time ago. In time, the school had attained a reputation as one of the town's top grammar schools, catering for both boys and girls, but in their respective halves. Edie had passed her 11+ and was in the lower school.

My surrogate mother insisted on me escorting my surrogate sister to and from school to home. Jackie Booth, who lived nearby, tagged along. Once across Free School Lane, it was a short walk to our terrace house in Ivy Street.

Ivy Street.

Of all the streets, Lorna had to choose a house in a street reminding me of my former wife. Edie told me we had moved here from Wyvern Place after our father had died. When I asked why, Edie explained in a quiet voice our mother could not cope with all the memories the old house held. It brought back too many sad memories of when our father was alive. Lorna had wanted a fresh start for the family. Edie snapped out of her sadness and immediately began trying to embarrass me in front of Jackie.

She insisted on telling Jackie all about some boy called Tom Catford, who lived on the street. Edie found it highly amusing telling Jackie all about how he had tried chatting me up, but I was too shy to talk to him. At least that's what Edie claimed. If her story was true, I had quite fancied him, a claim I was in no position to confirm or deny.

Most days, Edie told me, we would inevitably encounter some of the boys on our walk home. Today proved the first of some interesting occasions for me.

"Eh, up! It's long tall Shorty and her sister." A voice behind me called out. I turned around to find an acne-riddled youth with short fair hair accompanied by two other lads of about our age creeping up behind.

Jackie nearly jumped out of her skin. "Steve! I might have known it would be you'd be sneaking up behind us!"

The teasing began, aimed at me.

"Stories are doing the rounds about how you died in hospital and then came back from the dead," the boy Jackie identified as Steve began, his friends making ghostly accompanying noises, "is it true, Alice?"

Sizing him up, I knew from experience as a teenage boy there was no real harm in him. His manner was typical of an adolescent teenager on the verge of manhood. This young man was clueless and brusque in a puppy-dog kind of way. He had no real idea yet of how to deal with the opposite sex. I nodded in response but said nothing, finding our encounter humorous.

"So? What was it like being dead? Did you get to see the Pearly Gates? Or did you get Old Nick prodding you with his toasting fork?" He bantered, attempting a conversation. I confess I'd heard far worse chat-up lines as a man, even used some. Foolishly, I smiled back in response.

"Just leave her alone, Stingray." Jackie interceded on my behalf.

"Stingray?" I must have sounded surprised.

"That's my nickname, lass!" He confirmed proudly. "My name's Steven. Steve to my pals. I'm Steve Wray, but my mates all call me Stingray, like the telly program. Get it? Steve Wray. Stingray?"

I found myself laughing. I laughed, even more, when he cheekily asked me out in his broad Yorkshire accent. "How d'ya fancy going t'pictures with me on a date?"

This was my first experience of boys showing interest in me.

"Thanks for the invite, but no thanks," I replied politely. "Nice of you to ask, but you're not my type, Stingray."

He had the cheek to put his arm around me. "How do you know? I might be the boy of your dreams." His breath smelled of spearmint chewing gum.

"I don't think so!" I pushed him away from me, laughing.

The situation was as bizarre as it was unexpected. I had never considered the possibility a boy could be interested in me. When he slapped me on my bottom, I gasped in surprise and tried to slap him back. He'd anticipated my response moving out of the way swiftly. They found my shocked expression hilarious.

"Catch ya later, gorgeous!" He blew me a farewell kiss as he ran off ahead with the others laughing.

"He's always fancied you," Jackie sighed, barely hiding her feelings. "He's harmless as far as Lower Sixth boys go. You get a lot of horseplay with them around."

This was my first indication that Jackie liked him. Edie couldn't stop laughing. "Your face, Alice! Flash, bang, wallop! What a picture! Wish I'd had a camera. Your face! It was so funny!"

I didn't know what to say back to her. I must have gone red because the two of them laughed even more.

"He'd better not try it again! Or I'll...I'll slap his face raw, I'll..." Part of me was offended by the liberty he had taken. A part of me experienced something unexpected. I found myself strangely flattered by the attention, it left me feeling bothered and bewildered.

Edie was incapable of keeping quiet. No sooner had our mother returned from work than Edie recounted what had happened on the way home. I might add coloured with some gleeful exaggeration. Lorna had one of those immediate motherly concerned expressions on hearing Edie's tale. After all, I was seventeen going on eighteen, the age when girls were supposedly showing a keener than keen interest in the opposite sex. Later on in the evening, she took me aside. We had a chat, not so much about the birds and the bees, as about young men. I think I managed to show sufficient teenage embarrassment convincingly.

The seriousness I paid to her concerns about my virginity, she accepted with relief. When I explained I knew all about the facts of life already, she gave a visible sigh of relief. She was even more relieved when I added I had no intention of allowing anyone to make me pregnant.

"Alice, you've grown up so much since you were in the hospital. You've changed so fast, but at least now you're growing into a serious young woman. It's as though I have a new daughter." She kissed me affectionately on the forehead. How little did she know, and how right she was.

My automatic response was to hug and hold her close. Was my response prompted by guilt? Guilt because I had taken over her daughter's body? Or was it a genuine emotional and affectionate response? I knew I should be feeling guiltier than I did. For whatever reason I had come to possess Alice's body, I hoped I had not dispossessed her. Or worse still, that I had stolen her young life. Something more than a feeling within me suggested I hadn't.

It would be in another time and in another place when I would come to know for sure I hadn't.

My physical mother had passed away some years ago. So had my father. Neither had managed to reach retirement age. Both parents had passed away prematurely, dogged by ill-health. My father had worked at an asbestos plant. Asbestosis had inevitably caused his premature death.

Somewhere, I had an older brother. Michael had emigrated to Canada before the war. His letters home had become infrequent. Over time he stopped writing altogether. In some respects, I was equally poor at keeping in touch. To my knowledge, the seven years difference in our ages had made me feel less close. I could have done better and maybe written more often than I did. The war interrupted my letter writing. When I did write, there was no response. My letters started to return marked with no such person at this address. Perhaps he had served in the Canadian armed forces? Maybe he had died in the war? I never did find out.

My younger brother, Andrew, hadn't settled back into civilian life. The sea had lured him back, and so he had gone off to join the merchant navy. I know he came back once to see Ivy and Cathy after I died. That was the only visit for quite a few years.

It no longer mattered. I had inherited a new family and I intended to look after it with my life if necessary.

This may seem peculiar, but I had begun regarding Lorna Liddell as *my* mother. Alice's body seemed to tell my mind to accept I would always be her child, no matter who I thought I was or had been. Emotionally, I was drawn to her and beginning to love her as though I was her daughter. For Lorna, I would always remain her Alice, no matter how different I seemed. As for me? I was becoming someone else. From now on, I had to accept life as Alice, a young woman, and everything it would entail. My journey into acceptance of womanhood, I suppose, started then, at that moment. Henceforward I would embrace what the mirror showed me and what my new body told me.

One of the benefits of my past life had been the military discipline instilled in me by the army. Unlike Alice, who had been untidy, I was neat, disciplined, and organised. Everything had to have a place, and it needed to

37

be kept squared away. I performed my chores around the house, helping Lorna in every way I could. At the same time, as Edie's older sister, I wanted to set a positive example for her to follow. Surprisingly, Lorna and I saw a real change begin to take place in Edie. Within a fortnight, my transformation into Alice Mark II had become accepted. No matter how different I seemed, this Alice was still very much one of the Liddell's.

Chapter 7

You Can Make It If You Try – Yvonne Fair/James Brown
(King 45-5687 1962)

Friday, 7 October 1966

The next lesson after the morning break was PE. To say PE was unpopular with many of the girls was a proverbial understatement.

As a boy, I had happy memories of how my schoolmates looked forward to the lesson. Of course, there were always a couple of shirkers. Ones who did their best to get out of doing games. No one looked forward to the cross-country run around the parkland. Still, we got on with it. Rugby and football were always keenly contested and enjoyed. Our PE teacher brooked no-nonsense when it came to getting cleaned up at the end of the lesson. Girls, it appeared, were resistant to taking a shower.

My mindset at this point was still a little more male than female. I assumed, wrongly, that girls took personal hygiene more seriously than boys. No, they didn't. Not at school, not when it came to games. At first, I couldn't understand why, but it didn't take me long to learn why. There was an inbuilt fear having everything to do with girl's bodies. Anyone, even slightly plump, or with big, tiny, or uneven breasts, or with any other perceived bodily defect, became reluctant to reveal herself in the buff.

The changing room was far too small for the number of girls having to use it. This did not help where personal privacy was concerned. There was none. The usual excuse to avoid PE and not to shower was to claim it was the time of the month. Our teacher, although young, was neither inexperienced nor easily taken in by such excuses. She kept a record of girls using periods as an excuse to catch them out. Jackie made me laugh by telling me about one girl who claimed to have had periods on four consecutive lessons.

Something more I learned about Alice revealed how much she/I had already changed. Alice had done everything she could to keep her body hidden when in the changing room. My behaviour as the reborn Alice was the complete opposite.

At his stage of my new life, I was still thinking more like a man than a young woman. After years in the army, I no longer had any inhibitions about male changing rooms or showering facilities. Where taking a shower was concerned, I showed no sense of embarrassment. With nothing more than a small towel, I walked through the changing room to the shower stall. Showered I returned to my clothes to dry off. This, to the astonishment of those who remembered the Alice of old. When a couple of girls began tittering as I walked past, I tutted. My disdainful glance and adult-like comment, "Oh, grow up," instantly stopped their sniggering.

I was perhaps the slimmest girl in the class but with a shape in perfect proportion to my body. Okay, so my bust was tiny, compared to others in the group, but my breasts were perfectly formed. My hips were as shapely female as they came. Later, from Jackie, I learned quite a few of my classmates were envious of me because of my figure. Especially my legs, which appeared unbelievably long. A few girls had even commented that I had beautifully shaped legs. I had to agree with them. They were stunning if I say so myself. My legs became one of my best assets and helped to make my career as a model.

My appointment with the school's career officer came unexpectedly in the afternoon. I found myself summoned from my Geography lesson to the careers room. Entering the tiny box-shaped office, a grey-looking individual confronted me. When he peered over his half-moon spectacles, I must have made his day. From then on, he brightened considerably, becoming unusually interested in me, or rather in my attractive appearance.

Mr. W explained he was not the school's usual Careers Officer. His colleague was off ill, so he had been assigned to take over. A swift glance over the details in my file led to the opening questions. Had I received any replies to my UCCA application forms? The ones Alice had sent out. She had listed York, Leeds, Sheffield, and Manchester, as the universities where she had wanted to study English. All these, I noted, were a comfortable railway journey close to home. So far, nothing had dropped through the letterbox about the application. On paper, my prospective grades appeared good enough to get a place.

Mr. W continued. Did I have a career in mind until I married? If so, what?

My reaction to his patronising question astonished him.

"Why do you assume an intelligent young woman like me would only want a career until she married?" He had nothing much to say in reply except a surprised, mumbled apology that sounded condescendingly dishonest.

Inevitably he raised the matter of my amnesia. Had it had affected my life and schoolwork? It hadn't I answered scathingly. If anything, Alice's ability to learn had already begun to improve, especially since I had become her.

At this stage, I had given no thought to a future career. What he suggested next angered me. I laughed in his face when he suggested teaching or becoming a librarian as a possibility. My laughing at his suggestions was not well received. The comment I made next went down even less well.

"I may change my university degree course yet, and I will give serious consideration to careers in merchant banking, corporate management, or stockbroking. These will be on my list of possible future occupations. Teaching won't be among them, neither will becoming a librarian."

My response came without serious thought, prompted only by a desire to put *this man* in his place. I had no idea what I wanted to do.

The necessity of adapting to life as a young woman had so far made me live a sheltered existence. Now, feeling more secure in my identity, I wanted to start enjoying a more open life. In an all-girls school, I'd so far never experienced male chauvinism. Now it had confronted me, and I could feel the blood rushing through my veins making me seethe. Was this the downside of being a young woman in mid-twentieth-century Britain? Then I started to remember words spoken to Cathy by Ivy. Words I had never given thought to or contested as a father.

Ivy had hectored the child with constant critical comments. "You have to learn how to make a home for your future husband and your children. How else will you get yourself a decent man if you don't? You need to know how to cook and clean. Otherwise, what kind of a housewife will you make someone? *That's what we women do.*"

Yes. That's what we women are supposed to do, be homemakers, bred to be future mistresses of homes and hearths. Between motherhood and granny hood, we might contribute to the household having a part-time job. Women were made victims of their biology and paternalistic male thinking. Call me cynical with a hint of misandry. *The times they were a-changing.* I had no plans to conform, even if I had to lead my life as a woman.

Later in the afternoon, during the English Lit class, feminist outrage gripped the room. The teacher enlightened us about the lives of women in Jane Austen's time. When a woman married, her fortune and personal effects became the property of her husband under the law of coverture. For a few seconds, the classroom fell into a deathly disbelieving hush. Then outrage found voice among the girls. What followed directed the course of the rest of the discussion. The teacher seemed to enjoy stirring up a hornet nest of opinion. Not only did this enliven the lesson, but it also gave me a reality check. The words of protests issuing forth from the girls suddenly became personal. What I had come across earlier with the Careers Officer left me with plenty to think about. What would I confront in a male-dominated world?

Over the coming weeks, I realised the girls in the Sixth Form were eager to get good grades. All were encouraged by their parents to become achievers and to work towards academic success. Lorna wasn't the only parent keen to see her daughters do well.

Some parents pressured their daughters a little too hard. Almost as soon as I got to *know* my fellow students *again,* I became acutely aware of those with serious family issues. Pamela's parents had begun to drive her crazy with their expectations. The poor girl became tearful if she achieved any grade less than a B in her essays. Her parents expected her to go on to study Law. Why? Because her father was the Hardacre of Hardacre, Hardcastle, and Hewitt, solicitors in the town. He had ambitions for Pamela to become a barrister, which didn't agree with what Pamela wanted. She had other ideas about her future life. Nor was Pamela the only one.

In my previous life, I had come to understand the importance of carefully choosing what you did for a livelihood. Why I hadn't done so for myself at the time mystified me. Had it been the circumstances of the life I had lived? Or had it been my state of mind brought on by my wartime experiences? My old life should have died with my body. I intended it should stay dead with the body. In this rebirth, my thoughts absorbed all the possibilities a new and different future could offer. The way ahead seemed obvious. I had to make as much money as I could as soon as I could. Money was the great liberator. Maybe hearing The Beatles singing about *Money* had encouraged me to re-think my ambitions in more mercenary ways.

Yes. Money was the key to an independent life. Money unlocked all kinds of doors to make life easier and more satisfying. Once earned, having enough of the folding stuff would enable me to travel and see the world. As Phil, such a life had never been within reach. Now, as Alice, the precious gift of a second life promised possibilities. The problem facing me was how best to make such money to lead such a life. Not money for myself, I hasten to add but to help support my surrogate family and Cathy. I owed the Liddell's that much and more.

Chapter 8

Get A Job – The Silhouettes (Parlophone R4407 – 1968)

Saturday, 22 October 1966

When Cathy called for me during the half-term break, we went for a walk in Saville Park. After our walk we sat talking in my bedroom. Cathy continued to instruct me about what I needed to know as a female. Another afternoon we met in the town to check out clothes and shoes. We also spent time together in my old home, where I continued to learn all about makeup, clothes, and the world of the young. The Bush portable radio I had bought as her father played music that proved a revelation. Cathy taught me all about pop music and groups like The Beatles. I found myself embracing the sounds of the young wholeheartedly. It surprised me how much I enjoyed listening to the pop tunes coming over the airwaves. In my previous life, I had never paid attention to music. Music had been a background vagueness, something I had largely ignored. These days popular music sounded almost magical and mysterious. It made me feel excited to be young and alive.

In the coming weeks, I listened to all the pop music shows broadcast over the radio. It became a habit and went down well with Edie, who shared my newfound love of pop music. Tamla Motown records moved me the most, as did songs by singers like Otis Redding. I also loved the turmoil engendered in me by the sound of The Rolling Stones, The Kinks, and The Who. Music became a passion bringing Edie and myself closer together as sisters.

The half-term had signalled the approach of Christmas in a couple of months. The nights had turned darker earlier and the days greyer and colder. It was the time of year when having a cold or 'flu had begun making the rounds. Cathy had succumbed, and we could not meet in town on Saturday afternoon. Rather than stay home and put up with Edie going through one of her spells of giddy silliness, I decided to walk into town. Some time alone would do me good, and I had a purpose in doing so.

Lorna gave me six shillings and sixpence as pocket money each week. Alice had received the same amount, which she had been in the habit of saving half towards birthday and Christmas presents. I continued to do the same, saving as much money as I could. The opportunity to stroll around the shops alone allowed me to browse for possible Christmas presents. This way, I could make a list of what I might be able to afford to buy for Lorna, Edie, and Frank. I was also on the prowl looking for a Saturday job, although without much luck.

While wandering through the town's indoor Victorian market, a woman stallholder on a fabrics counter gave me a peculiar look. She scrutinised my face with narrowed eyes making me pause.

"Pardon me for asking, but aren't Lorna Liddell's daughter?" The question took me by surprise.

"Why, yes," I answered, bewildered by her question. How did she know me?

"I thought I recognised you. It's been a while since I saw you last. I've heard you've lost your memory, so I suppose you won't remember me. I'm Angie's aunt, her Aunt Thelma."

That's how I came to reacquaint myself with the Thornton's. She asked after Lorna and apologised for not coming to see her. From her rambling, often disjointed conversation, I learned Angie's mother had been unwell for some time. This was one of the several reasons why she had not visited Lorna for so long. Thelma's sister's illness was proving a difficult time for her two daughters, Gillian and Angela. After a while, she eventually scribbled down an address to pass on to my mother, which I never thought to glance at. Perhaps, if Lorna was to visit Dolores, it might help her? Dolores? What a peculiar name? And so, this one-way conversation meandered on as I stood there listening for the better part of twenty minutes.

Eventually, I tried politely to tear myself away, explaining I needed to go home. My efforts proved a failure. There was no stopping, Thelma. By now, I was sure she could put a glass eye to sleep. Then out of the blue came the first of two pieces of information to fill in my backstory as Alice.

Angie's mum had given birth to her the same week Lorna had given birth to Alice. Slightly less than seven days separated the girls' arrivals. So, this was how the two had become friendly. The two mums had met one another on the maternity ward. Afterwards, they had kept up the friendship meeting regularly until recent events had overtaken their lives. Lorna had lost her husband, and Dolores had suffered her breakdown.

Finally, as exasperation was getting the better of me, Thelma asked if I was searching for work. I explained I was still at school but desperately seeking a Saturday job to earn some money. My strained patience found itself unexpectedly rewarded. One of her friends worked at Boots. She was

44

looking for a girl to work as a customer assistant on Saturdays. Inadvertently, I had stumbled by chance on a job. Better still, it came with a personal recommendation.

Thelma wrote a second brief note explaining I was a family friend of good character and looking for a Saturday job. With her recommendation in my hand, she told me to rush there. Otherwise, someone else might land the position before I had a chance. It proved my lucky day. I did as she suggested. Within half an hour, I had landed the job, which paid 10 shillings.

Curiosity had the better of me after I left Boots feeling jubilant. Who was this friend of mine called Angie? Instead of making my way to the bus station, something prompted me to make a snap decision. Before heading home, I would walk to George Square to the chemist's shop where this Angie worked. I wanted to take a look at this long-standing childhood friend of mine. The decision was spontaneous and made for no other reason than sheer curiosity.

George Square appeared surprisingly busy. A lot of young people my age were hanging around there. They seemed to be idling, talking in small groups, or larking about with one another. Later I would learn the Square was a meeting place for teenagers who called themselves Mods. They seemed to be mainly young men, but there were a few girls there too. One larger group I passed had gathered by parked scooters near the Black Swan Passage entrance. Little did I realise at the time how soon I would become one of their number.

The chemist shop, located in the newish building, was a little way up George Square, leading to the roundabout. The streetlights were already on as I made my way there. All I wanted to do was to see what this mysterious person looked like.

Through the window, I caught sight of her standing behind the counter. The chemists was empty. Truthfully, I have to say, she appeared to be in a world of her own, fed up and bored. Hardly surprising, there seemed nothing much to keep her occupied. She was like a beautiful doll with a blank expression, waiting for something to happen. I couldn't help thinking how dazzling she looked. Dark hair, striking dark eyes in a pale and alluring face, Angie Thornton was prettiness personified. Our eyes met, and I could see her gasp in delighted surprise. I turned to walk away and caught sight of her rushing to the door.

"Alice! Hang on! Please wait," I heard her call from the doorway. Her words made me stop and turn to meet her. She rushed out, uncertain how to greet me, and then threw her arms around me. "Alice, I'm so happy to see you. Edie told me you'd lost your memory. How are you? Has your memory come back?"

I shook my head, looked into her eyes, and knew instinctively from her gaze we were friends of long-standing. Even then, I sensed we would be friends once more, as Alice had been with Angie. This inexplicable awareness touched me so deeply it seemed almost magical.

We quickly arranged to meet after Sunday lunch. She would walk up to my home in Ivy Street, and then we'd walk back to her house in Manor Drive. We lived so close to one another, yet neither of us had known how close. I could not believe we had not run into one another until today.

Chapter 9

In My Life – The Beatles (Rubber Soul LP. Parlophone PMC 1267 – 1965)

Sunday, 23 October 1966

Angie called for me at three as arranged. Edie and my mother were delighted and excited to see her again after such a long time. It took the better part of a half-an-hour to pull ourselves away.

What did I make of this girl, who everyone liked? She was friendly, with a lively, engaging personality. I warmed to her even more as we walked and talked.

The Thornton's home was an impressive double fronted terrace with three floors. Built from local sandstone, it had a large garden to one side. Her father, she told me, had done very well for himself in the last few years. A green Triumph Herald stood parked at the rear. To my astonishment, Angie let me know the car belonged to her. She had passed her driving test during the summer.

What I liked most about their home was the location. A two-minute walk brought you to the open space of Manor Heath Park. From there, it was another short walk to Skircoat Green and the hospital. The same hospital where my mother had given birth to me, and Lorna to Alice. It also shared the distinction where Alice and I both died and where I had been reborn. The walk to Angie's home had taken less than ten minutes.

Another young woman greeted me as we arrived at the house. At a glance, I could tell this was her older sister, Gillian. Gill, as she preferred to be called, looked like an older version of Angie. They shared the same dark hair, eyes, and pale complexion.

Gill was now a nurse and remembered me as her sister's childhood friend. She knew all about my amnesiac condition and loss of memory. Angie had forewarned her, which was why Gill made no attempt to ask if I remembered her. Their mother, she explained, was upstairs heavily tranquilized and would be resting for an hour or two, probably longer. Given her state of mind today, it would be better not to disturb her. Excusing herself, saying how lovely it was to see me again, Gill explained she had some studying to do. Without another word, she smiled and quietly left us to spend time together.

47

"Gill and I are really close," Angie confessed. "We're not just sisters, we're great friends even though Gill is so much older. I don't know where I'd be if it wasn't for her."

The front room was tastefully furnished. I immediately recognised the modern G Plan coffee table. Lorna loved G Plan and would have furnished our home with the same had she the means. There was an Ercol sideboard like the one Ivy had tried to persuade me to buy when I was alive. The price had put me off. When Angie said her father had been doing well for himself, she had not been joking. Their home had fitted carpets. There was fine anaglypta patterned wallpaper on the walls and ceilings. Central heating radiators kept the house warm. It all looked so pristine and so comfortable.

In one way, I was dreading how our conversation would go. In another, I was intrigued. My adult male mind had soon realised how teenage girls and women were different from men. Women and girls loved talking with one another in ways men don't or couldn't. Unlike men and boys, with their urge to try to be the top dog in the pack, women and girls are different. Women and girls seemed more interested in establishing cosy friendly relationships. Co-operation, not competition was what I quickly understood differentiated women from men.

My short time as a female so far made me further appreciate why the genders were so different. Living as a teenage girl, I had become caught up in their world and topics of conversation. Teenage girls were gregarious. They loved to talk about boys and pop stars. Clothes, makeup, and gossip came a close second, matched by their obsession with weight problems. In this new world where I found myself, I knew I had to adapt and socialise to survive just to appear normal. Burying myself in a masculine shroud made no sense whatsoever if I wanted to have a life.

As a female, I also found myself eating far less than I had as a man. There was no way my female body could cope with the portions I had once eaten as a man. This, perhaps, proved one of the more difficult things I had to learn to do. I had always enjoyed eating. It hadn't taken me long to appreciate how eating and keeping a trim figure meant sticking to a mean lean eating regime.

For a few, dieting had already become an obsessive preoccupation, one I found myself hearing about all too regularly. Two girls in the Sixth Form had already been diagnosed with anorexia. Memories of Ivy grumbling about putting on weight and struggling to get into her girdle served as a reminder of the potential consequences. I had no intentions of ending up like Ivy, nor had I any intentions of becoming skeletal. I was already skinny enough.

As we chatted, food came up as a topic when we sat down for tea and biscuits. Neither of us was too fussy about what we liked to eat.

My chatter with Angie in the afternoon proved both revealing and disturbing. We had so much catching up to do, and she had a great deal to get off her mind. My new friend told me she wished she had listened to me, or rather to Alice. Angie told me she had come to bitterly regret leaving school and wasting her opportunities. Apparently, Alice had tried everything to persuade her to stay on but had failed.

Foolishly, Angie had become involved with a twenty-two-year-old man who had seduced her and taken her virginity. He had been the one who had tempted her to leave school with all kinds of promises. This man, who she identified as Ray, had taken to slapping her around when she wouldn't do as he wanted. When she broke free of him, it was with the help of one of his friends, someone she referred to as Eric. Eric was as bad as Ray. He only wanted her for sex. In the end, her Uncle Den had learned what was going on from Gill and intervened. It had been quite a violent intervention.

Den had then hunted down this Ray bloke. He had given him one hell of a beating resulting in hospitalisation. The bloke had kept quiet, refusing to tell the police anything. Otherwise, he would have gone to jail for having had sex with an underage girl. Had her sister not found out, goodness knows what more could have happened to Angie. Gill had been the one to appeal to Den for help rather than to her father. Matters would have gotten completely out of hand if her father had become involved.

Den, Angie told me, had been a Teddy Boy back in his youth and still looked the part with his greased quiff. Even though he was married with young children, he still loved to don his draped jacket and drainpipe trousers. As a young man, Den had frequent brushes with the law. One had led to a short stay in borstal.

Angie's story made me appreciate how vulnerable and impressionable young women could be. They seemed to succumb too readily to the charms of anyone they believed to be more mature. Since her awful experiences, Angie told me she had grown wary of boys and men. She admitted what a hard and cruel series of lessons she had had to learn.

Curiosity got the better of me and I had to ask about the car. Her grandfather on her mum's side left Gill and her some money in his will. Against her dad's better advice, Den had agreed to give Angie driving lessons. He had found her this second-hand low mileage Triumph Herald and she had learned to drive in the car. With his help, she had passed her driving test.

Angie loved motoring. She told me how she had gone to Blackpool on the August Bank holiday weekend, having passed the driving test the week before. I didn't realise at the time how obsessed Angie was going to be with motor cars later in life.

The conversation moved on with Angie wanting to know all about her old classmates. That proved easy enough as the girls in my form had become so familiar, welcoming, and friendly on my return. I'd quickly learned all their names. After my run-ins with Janice Barrowclough, my popularity had grown. Whether this was to stay on my good side, I wasn't sure. A few had genuinely become much friendlier. Angie almost fell about laughing when I told her about my exchanges with Barrowclough.

Before I knew what was what, I found Angie had decided I should have my fingernails manicured by her. This was something else I was starting to understand about being female. We were so much more touchy-feely than men. Reluctantly I agreed to let her paint my nails a pearl colour. As she did so, my reluctance slipped away. The experience was strangely pleasant and a feminine way to bond our friendship. I had to admit I liked the way my fingernails looked when she finished. Like wearing makeup, it was something else I would need to master.

Angie insisted on showing me the dresses she had bought. So, we went up to her bedroom. This was larger than the one I shared with Edie. Wallpapered in a pink and white pattern, a chintzy white dressing table with a matching chintzy mirror stood against the wall. Next to it, she had a matching white wardrobe. In the corner of the room was a chair full of stuffed toys. The bedroom was about as feminine as it could get and reflected her personality.

The wardrobe had reached a bursting point, overflowing with dresses and coats. Angie admitted she was fortunate and spoiled. At the chemists, she earned £5 a week. Her father didn't expect her to pay her keep. A fiver wasn't a fortune. For a girl of her age, it was a great deal of money. Angie also told me how her father would often slip her a pound or two extra on the side for clothes or petrol.

Fashion was an aspect of my life as a young woman I had not yet begun to appreciate. Not until this visit to Angie's. In the next hour or so, she dragged me into a world about which I knew little or nothing. The way she spoke about clothes made me realise how little I understood their importance to a young woman. The next hour changed me. She made me try one of her dresses, then another, then another. Before long I must have tried most of the dresses and skirts. A burgundy coloured short-sleeved sheath dress I tried had three-inch slits at each side. Slightly taller than her, the hemline came four inches above my knees. I had to admit, seeing myself in Angie's mirror, I did look attractive in it.

"Do you like this one?" She asked.

"I do," I cooed in surprise, astonished at the sound my voice had made on seeing myself.

"I'd like you to have it, Alice."

No matter how I tried to refuse her kind offer, she became even more insistent, pointing to the wardrobe and its bulging contents. "I need to make space for more. Besides, it looks so much better on you than me."

In the end, I gave in. Angie said I was stunning and model material. Little did I appreciate how important this one moment would prove and how it would determine my future.

Angie told me she was a Mod. Mod fashions changed quickly. Mods she told me, loved to dress fashionably and to look sharp and chic. Fashion was a passion. If you were a Mod, your mission in life was to look stylish and to have a good time all the time. This, she told me firmly, was the only way to live. Life as a Mod was all about having fun.

I remembered reading about Mods and Rockers in the newspapers. There had been some brawling in several seaside resorts on the South Coast a few years ago. It had caused a minor uproar in the press at the time, not that I had taken much notice. Some weird headline came back to memory. Someone had described the youths involved as Sawdust Caesars.

"Aren't Mods always fighting with these Rockers?" My curiosity had been aroused by the memory of the fighting on Brighton beach.

"Good heavens, no!" She let out a small laugh. "You don't want to believe what you read in the newspapers. It happened a few years ago. I've never heard of any of the local lads getting into fights with any Rockers. We never see any Greasers around here. They stay away from the town centre."

Angie then asked if I would like to go dancing at a club in the town on Saturday night. The club was the same one Cathy kept mentioning, The Plebeians or The Plebs. I said I would think about it, but what was there to think about? Nothing. Now I was a teenager, the second time around, the idea appealed even more. Why shouldn't I start enjoying my life and behave as a young person living in the nineteen-sixties? Besides, when Angie told me about the music they played, it sounded perfect. The next thing I knew,

51

out came a small, portable record player from under the bed. We started to listen to some of her collection of best-loved 45s as we chatted. Angie came alive her eyes were shining, and keen to talk about her favourite records.

The record labels had me fascinated. Intriguing names like $tateside, printed with a dollar sign. I already knew some of the Motown acts like *The Four Tops* and *The Supremes.* Angie introduced me to names like *Jackie Wilson, The Fascinations, The Drifters, Sam & Dave,* and *Otis Redding,* to name only a few. She had around fifty 7" singles. They must have cost her a small fortune to buy. A single 45 record cost about 6s 6d, which was my weekly pocket money.

During our talking, I managed to ask Angie about her memories of the two of us when we were younger. From the chair filled with stuffed toys, she brought me a small black cat. Apparently, I had given her the stuffed toy on her tenth birthday. It had been a gift she had always treasured and reminded her of me, or rather Alice.

"You gave me this and said you hoped it would always bring me luck. You said black cats were supposed to be lucky. We named it Whisper."

I found myself deeply moved by Angie's touching words. She recounted various incidents from different times in our childhood years. As she told me more about her friendship with Alice, sadness and regret filled my thoughts for the Alice she had lost. Still, I knew this was a friendship I would keep up and not simply in memory of the real Alice. Here was someone who wanted to be my friend and, I had to admit, someone I instinctively liked for who she was. Glancing at her alarm clock, I couldn't believe how the hours had passed and how much I had enjoyed spending time with her. Whatever it took, I promised myself I would do everything in my power to maintain our friendship. I need not have worried. Angie intended we should renew our friendship. She was also insistent we should go down The Plebs on a Saturday night.

Angie had gone through more than her share of teenage angst by the time she was sixteen. More than most from her previous admissions. Then she chose to make a further strange confession, leaving me even more fascinated.

A while ago, she had met a boy. One who had captivated her so much at first sight she had fallen for him.

James MacKinnon was Tom Catford's cousin. Tom was one of her close friends among the local Mods. Not another coincidence, I couldn't help thinking. The boy from Wyvern Place. And the name MacKinnon sounded familiar too. This cousin's nickname was Mack. Mack now lived in Bradford but had once lived nearby. He had travelled over on his scooter to go to the club with Tom. Angie said she had fallen for him at first sight, even having had sex with him the same night, which fact left me stunned. It had been his first time. She had seduced him. At the time, Angie told me she thought it was going to be a one-time-lust-driven mad fling.

What had taken her so much by surprise was what a lovely person this young man turned out. How much he had respected her, and every time they met after afterwards. Now, whenever she saw him, she wanted to be with him, even though she knew he had a girlfriend. Angie had made a brave decision. She told me she would not attempt to steal him away from his girlfriend, although she had been tempted. What she had heard from Mack about her rival had made her heartache for them both.

I listened to her recount the story of how the two had become separated by her parents. The pair had continued to meet one another in secret. Quite a romantic tale, almost a Mod tale of Romeo and Juliet on a scooter. After hearing the story, my sympathy still lay with Angie. Her frustrated love affair I could easily relate to and understand. When I eventually met Mack and his girlfriend, I appreciated Angie's situation better.

As I listened, I did not know then this young man, his girlfriend, and Angie would change my life forever, including their own.

When we came downstairs, I heard a gruff voice. It sounded strangely familiar. I couldn't place when or where I'd heard it before. Another male voice replied, and the two men began to guffaw. Angie and I spoke in whispers as I put my duffle coat on, wrapping my scarf around my neck, bracing myself for the cold outside. The Thornton's enjoyed the luxury of central heating, and what a luxury and pleasure it had been to experience the warmth. I wasn't looking forward to being greeted by the cold when I left.

"It's my dad and my Uncle Den. I suppose you had better say hello to them before you go," Angie suggested awkwardly. I followed her into the living room, and my heart almost stopped. No wonder the voice sounded familiar. So, it should have. I had spent most of the war listening to its bark. I came face to face with my past. Sergeant-Major Bill Thornton and I had served together during the war in the same regiment.

Chapter 10

Reflections – The Supremes (Tamla Motown TMG 616 –1967)

Sunday, 23 – Wednesday, 26 October 1966

Briefly, I'd wondered if Angie could be related to my old army comrade. Thornton was a common enough name in Yorkshire, but I had dismissed the idea once I met Angie. Neither she nor her sister Gill looked anything like him. Later I would learn something of their mother's Maltese ancestry. Their dark brown eyes and black hair contrasted with his greying brown hair and hazel eyes. Which was why seeing him again came like an exploding artillery shell out of nowhere.

For a moment or so, I thought he was about to call out Phil as he looked me over, delighted to see me. Then it struck me. He wasn't seeing Phil Manley but his daughter's friend.

"Hello, Alice. Tha's shot up, lass, since I last saw thee," he boomed in his broad Yorkshire accent.

I nodded dumbfounded, unsure how to reply. Angie intervened on my behalf, reminding him I had lost my memory.

Though we lived in the town, we'd not seen one another since our demob. Our discharge papers had arrived sooner than we expected. We'd had no opportunity to let our families know we were coming home, so no one was there to greet our return as our train had pulled into the station.

The relief and joy we had as we stepped out onto the platform left the pair of us grinning like idiots. What heady feelings we enjoyed knowing we had survived the war to make it home. Now the strangeness of Civvy Street struck home as we left the station and made our way up the hill on Horton Street. When Bill and I reached the corner of Market Street, we stopped. There, shaking hands, we made vague comradely promises to meet up sometime in a local pub and parted company. Bill Thornton turned off on Union Street while I made my way to Ward's End in search of a bus home. That had been twenty or more years ago.

Angie wanted to walk me back, at least part of the way. No sooner outside than her words caught me off guard.

"Is your memory coming back?" She asked with genuine excitement. "You looked as if you'd remembered my dad when he spoke to you."

54

A denial was out of the question. Angie had seen the surprise on my face. I had been unable conceal the shock of seeing him again, and now could not deny the fact. So once again, I had to pretend.

"His face seemed so familiar, as though I had met him somewhere before," I replied, trying to sound vague and uncertain, yet in my own way being truthful.

"Oh! Perhaps your memory is starting to come back to you?" Angie was genuinely thrilled. In the end, she walked me more than halfway home chatting happily. Even if I'd had ulterior motives to be her friend, I left her knowing I genuinely wanted to rekindle Alice's old friendship. Of course, for me, it would be a new friendship built on a deception, but my feelings were genuine. I sensed instinctively we had a true and lasting friendship in the making, and my instinct was not wrong.

On the way home, I arrived at a decision. I resolved to mention things I had learned from others about Alice's life. In this way, dishonestly, I would give my new family hope my memories might return someday.

Frank was working outside as I came home, trying to fix something on his motorcycle. The Francis Barnett Falcon was his one prized possession. Lorna had helped him to buy the six-year-old machine so he could travel to work in Elland. I knew a little about motorcycles, having owned an AJS after I came out of the army. But now, as a girl, I couldn't help him. It would have been far too strange. As a schoolgirl, I was not supposed to know anything about motorcycle maintenance or mechanics.

"What's wrong, Frank?" I asked.

Frank scratched his head as he looked up at me. He was at a loss to explain why the engine would not start. The spark plug, and the carburettor jets, had been cleaned, and nothing. The engine remained dead. The tank was full, so a lack of petrol was not the cause of the fault. Even trying to jump-start a couple of times had failed to get the engine going.

I couldn't pretend ignorance any longer. I offered a casual suggestion. Was the battery working? Was the electric charge getting through to the engine? Frank gave me a strange look and began to check the battery terminals. He emitted a loud snort and smacked the side of his head. From his tool kit, he took a spanner and tightened the battery terminals. The engine sprang to life on the third kick.

"Sis, you're brilliant. I don't know why I didn't think to check the terminals. The cable on the positive was loose!" He chuckled, his head slumping, his features relaxing as he released a huge sigh. Frank switched the engine off then and pulled the bike onto its stand. He came over to me and gave me a peck on the forehead, taking care not to get his dirty hands on my clothes. "Thanks for spotting the obvious, Alice. I was panicking, wondering how I was going to get to Elland in the morning."

"What was the problem?" My pretence at ignorance brought a smile to his face.

"One of the battery leads had slackened and was loose. The electrical charge wasn't getting to the spark plug. Your guess was right."

After tea, I helped to wash and tidy up, as a good daughter should. Then I got down to finishing my English Lit homework seated at the kitchen table. Edie interrupted me ten minutes later, wanting help with her maths. By nine o'clock, I was in bed reading *Hamlet* for tomorrow's English lesson. Edie was avidly reading an old copy of Lorna's *Women's Own*.

"Why do we have periods?" She asked, interrupting my reading.

I sighed, stopped reading, and did my best to explain.

"But it's no use now," thought poor Alice,
"To pretend to be two people!
Why, there's hardly enough of me left
to make one *respectable person!"*

Lewis Carroll 'Alice in Wonderland'

Chapter 11

I Don't Need No Doctor – Ray Charles (HMV POP 1566 – 1966)

Monday 31, October 1966

Lorna insisted we kept the appointment with the psychiatrist. My attempts to get out of attending failed miserably.

"Resistance is useless!" Edie teased, doing a passable Doctor Who Dalek impression. With considerable reluctance, I found myself having to attend the appointment.

The brass nameplate on the door announced Dr. K. Piller, Psychiatrist. She greeted me as we entered her office, which was nothing like a typical consulting room. I had half expected to find a psychiatrist's couch and someone resembling Herbert Lom in TV's *The Human Jungle*. Instead, there were two bright red mushroom chairs with a small coffee table in an otherwise almost empty room. On the table was a battery-operated tape recorder bearing the words Stellaphone ST470. Against one wall stood a bookcase filled with loose-leaf binders and file boxes rather than books

The psychiatrist asked Lorna to wait outside while I had my session. She had to be about the same age as Lorna. Her plain grey two-piece suit concealed a white turtleneck top. Sitting down she crossed her legs, her nylon stockings rubbing together made a slight hiss.

Dr. Piller then invited me with a silent gesture to sit down in the other chair. I was pleasantly surprised to discover how comfortable and relaxing the chair was, my hands enjoying the soft texture of the fine wool covering. She studied me in silence as I tried to relax and prepare for the questions. Her stare was uncomfortable, somewhere between weird and creepy. It left me with an uneasy sensation as she cleared her throat. She flicked the switch on the tape recorder and began.

"Who are you?"

What a strange question to ask?

"I don't really know," I replied. "I used to know, but things have changed since then. Now, I don't remember, and I'm no longer sure."

"What do you mean by that?" Dr. Piller asked with evident sternness, observing me closely with steely grey eyes. "Explain yourself, Alice."

"I can't because I have no idea who I was, and I am not entirely sure who I am now. I have no memories of who Alice used to be. I only know who I am now."

There was no point pretending to be two people. My original self would have to make one new Alice. I would do this with the help of recollections from others.

Dr. Piller appeared intrigued by my response and commenced plying me with a continuous stream of questions. Did I remember anything? Did I have dreams about my life before my clinical death and resuscitation? Did I remember anything during death? On and on. No sooner was one question answered than she began with another, ticking off my answers on a xeroxed sheet. When I thought the questioning was over, she would start with a new batch turning over to yet another sheet.

How did I now feel about what had happened to me? How did I feel about being alive? How did my classmates and teachers treat me? I had come with a plan and did my utmost to stick to it. My responses became littered with scattered anecdotes I had picked up from my family and friends about Alice. I was hoping it would lend some authenticity to the possibility my memory might be returning. At the end of the session, I waited outside while Lorna spoke in private with the doctor.

When she left the office with Dr. Piller, they were smiling. I was in for several surprises.

"I've arranged to see you once a month for therapy sessions," the good doctor announced with her serious face, "so we can try to restore more of your memory. I'll make an appointment for you with my secretary and send a letter to your mother."

Frankly, I was stunned. My hopes for a cursory visit requiring no further appointments were dashed. The last thing I needed was someone prying about in my head.

"I don't want my lessons at school disrupting," I prefaced my response, "and I don't want to lose any more time."

"That's fine, Alice. I will make sure all the appointments are after school hours." The doctor replied with the most synthetic of smiles.

Before I could respond further, Lorna addressed Dr. Piller. "Thank you for what you are doing for Alice. It is so lovely to see you again after so many years, Katie."

"And so lovely to meet you again, Lorna. It has been quite a while, more time than I care to recall," Doctor Piller responded with an even more plastic smile.

Great. The two knew one another. This was what I did not want to hear. As we walked home, Lorna told me she and Katie had attended the same primary school. Katie had been the brightest pupil in the class and had gone on to the grammar school. One interesting comment Lorna made was how surprised she was that Katie now dyed her hair blonde. She had been a dull mousy brunette as a child. Blondes have more fun, was my response, although there was nothing fun about Katie Piller.

If I didn't take care, Katie Piler could cause me a few problems. Nor did I like the idea of her tape recording the session. Taping our conversations had me worried. Before I met her next, I would have to learn as much as I could about Alice's early life. If I could prove my memory was returning, I might not need to come back. All I needed to do was keep up a steady flow of stories about her life before the amnesia. Only then, I might convince Katie Piler I no longer needed her services. If I did this, it would help to keep my true self secret. From now on, I would need to be on my guard during our encounters.

Chapter 12

Sho 'Nuff Got A Good Thing Goin' – J.J. Jackson
(Warner Brothers WB 2082 – 1967)

Tuesday, 15 November 1966

Pamela and Marjorie, who were in our form, had befriended me. We had never been especially friendly, but we had all got on well with one another. Or so Jackie led me to believe. She seemed pleased they wanted to be in our circle as friends. The two girls were good fun as it happened. During morning break they unintentionally helped to fill in some important gaps in Alice's missing history. Pamela, the curly-haired, blonde managed to make my cheeks burn.

"We saw you a couple of times, talking to a boy from Heath Grammar after school," she teased, a large smile forming as she looked towards Marjorie for support, "didn't we, Marjorie?"

Marjorie nodded, beaming, then winked at Jackie. "He couldn't take his eyes off you, Alice. You were blushing like mad as the two of you walked down Skircoat Green Road."

I glanced at Jackie, who shrugged her shoulders in response before asking the question I wanted to have answered. "When was this?"

The two girls exchanged looks, frowning as if trying to recall the exact day and time.

"I think it was just before you went into the hospital," Pamela replied, narrowing her gaze. Turning to Marjorie, she asked, "Or was it?"

Marjorie seemed puzzled, replying a second or two later, "Now you mention it, I'm sure it was the second time. Possibly the day when you collapsed."

"Do you know who he was?" The incident had aroused my curiosity instantly. According to my sister and Jackie, I had never had a boyfriend. Both claimed I was far too shy of the opposite sex. Their unfolding tale made me curiouser and curiouser.

"Brenda might know." Pamela mused momentarily. "Brenda saw you with him. She said you were at the post office when she bumped into you."

"I'll go and get her, shall I?" Volunteered Marjorie. "The nosey mare will know exactly where and when it all happened."

Brenda, the Sixth Form's gossip, had made it her mission in life to know all about everyone's business. Being a nosey parker was her downside. Brenda's upside was she knew everything about everyone when it came to gossip, even more so if it involved scandal. If you wanted to know the latest spicy titbits, then Brenda was your girl. Like the others in my year, she knew all about my amnesia and lost memory. When I asked her about this boy I had been seen with, she took great pleasure in enlightening them and me. Naturally, Brenda knew all about him. That was how I came to know about Terry Hare.

Terry, she told me, was a choice dish. He was in the Upper Sixth at Heath Grammar. Brenda had seen me chatting to him at the post office. We had also been seen walking through the park. Then came the information I wasn't expecting. Terry had been the one who had called for the ambulance when Alice had collapsed. Or that was what I thought.

All this was news to me. Probably to Lorna, too, since her and Frank's version made no mention of him. In their version of events, I had collapsed in the street by the library. Some passers-by had made a 999 call from the library. Who these passers-by were, they had no idea? We never found out. They had supposed some local, good Samaritans. The police had called at the house shortly after the hospital had notified them of Alice's arrival. Her address and details had been written on the inside of her satchel. The one I used now.

I knew from what Lorna had told me Alice had been unconscious on arrival at the Infirmary. She never recovered consciousness. Alice had died in the emergency ward around the same time I died. Lorna and Edie had arrived minutes before it happened. Frank had rushed from work, arriving as the doctor was informing Lorna. Since there had been no autopsy due to my revival as Alice, I could not help wondering what had caused her death?

Did this boy, Terry Hare, know what had happened to her? If he was present when she collapsed, he could have some idea what may have caused it. Once this thought occurred, I could not let it go. An unfounded suspicion started taking shape as I listened. Was he in some way responsible for Alice's death?

The day after, Brenda was waiting for me at the school entrance as I approached with Jackie. Fortunately for me, Edie had rushed ahead to walk with some girls from her form. Otherwise, hearing anything about this boy would get straight back to Lorna. Not that Edie was a snitch. She simply could not keep her mouth shut, especially if she had an opportunity to embarrass her big sister.

"Guess what?" Brenda began, pleased with what she knew. "I saw him yesterday on my way home. I stopped and talked with Terry. I told him you'd been asking about him."

"Oh?" Brenda's words took me by surprise. My guarded response in a matter-of-fact manner attempted to show disinterest.

"Terry said he didn't know you had almost died in hospital. Or that you'd got amnesia. Or that you didn't know who you were when they brought you around. He seemed surprised when I told him."

"And did he say anything when you told him?" I kept quiet about how I'd revived on the way to the mortuary.

"Yes, he did!" Brenda almost squealed in her excitement. "He asked me to ask you if he could see you again. There's a party at someone's house. Not this weekend. The weekend after. He wants you to come, and he wants me to get some of our friends to go too."

Jackie looked at me. Unsure what to say, I replied, "I don't know if my mum will let me go." It was unexpected, but it didn't faze Brenda.

"It'll be fab. You two have to go. I'll be going. I can't pass up a chance like this. Besides, I think you should go, Alice. He wants to see you again," Brenda babbled, "and Pamela will go when she knows about the party. And where Pamela goes, Marjorie goes too. June will want to go, and so will her friend Nancy, in the Fifth Form."

Jackie said nothing. She was downcast, and I understood why. Unlike the other girls in our year, Jackie was a late developer. Physically, she was so tiny one of the new teachers had mistaken her for a Second Former. The poor girl had suffered a lot of teasing after the incident. During the morning break, I asked if she wanted to go to the party with me.

Jackie shook her head. "I would love to go, but my mum wouldn't let me. Besides I have nothing nice to wear. My mum makes me wear clothes like the ones first formers wear. I'm so tiny she buys clothes sized for eleven and twelve-year-olds."

Hearing Jackie say this was heart-breaking. I put my arm around her and gave her a squeeze and a smile. "Come round to my house. We'll see what Edie has that you could borrow."

I knew I had to go to the party.

It hadn't taken me long to adjust to the novelty of school life the second time around, even if it was as a teenage girl.

Grammar schoolgirls were nothing like grammar schoolboys. Certainly not going by my pre-war school experiences. Most girls were much more diligent and presented the teachers with far fewer problems. I had advantages over all the girls in my groups. Another lifetime's hard-earned experiences and knowledge as a former adult male gave me numerous advantages.

Alice had a reputation for drifting off and daydreaming in lessons. She had never presented the teachers with any discipline problems. On the contrary. From her past school reports, every teacher regarded her as a well-behaved, pleasant, and polite pupil. The only common complaint shared by her teachers had been about her occasional daydreaming or inattentiveness. The new Alice they were dealing with was entirely different. My teachers had grown more circumspect about this Alice since her return to school.

Brenda's news this morning had distracted me. A frisson of unexpected sensation had flooded me when I heard of Terry Hare's interest. In one way, I found the thought distasteful. Yet in another, strangely thrilling. My mind said one thing. My body was telling me another.

One of the many things I was learning about teenage girls was how obsessed they were with boys. I was now getting a taste of what they were experiencing. I should have known why, but I had yet to understand the reasons for it. There was one thing I had quickly learned when eavesdropping on girls' conversations.

Teenage girls fell into and out of love at the drop of a tear-stained handkerchief.

Chapter 13

Living To Please – Dolores Clark f. Ray Starling (Antares AX 101 - 1966)

Thursday 17 – Saturday 19, November 1966

"You're seventeen, almost eighteen, and a young woman." Lorna passed me a small package. "It's about time you dressed liked one. They'll expect you to look the part this Saturday when you start work. You can't keep wearing knee socks when you're nearly eighteen. The time has come to start wearing stockings."

Great. I suppose it was inevitable. The girls in the Sixth all wore them, so did most in the Fifth. Only Jackie and I didn't. In Jackie's case being so tiny, presented size issues. For most girls wearing stockings, like wearing a bra, was about moving into womanhood.

So far, I had avoided the suspender belt in my underwear drawer. Inevitably I would have to start wearing stockings. Alice had worn them, but as yet, I had not, finding the idea strangely embarrassing. It had to be an inevitable next step and unavoidable. A part of me still harboured reservations about putting on stockings and suspenders. It was silly, really. I had overcome my reservations about wearing female attire out of necessity.

Underwear and a skirt had come relatively painlessly. A brassiere, less so. Since Alice didn't own any trousers or ski pants, I had no choice. It was a skirt or a dress, or nothing. They were a necessity, and I had adapted to these quicker than I thought. I needed reminding to wear a slip. From a female point of view, I understood the practicality of a slip. Suspenders? Stockings? These were something else. The thought of wearing them made me feel like a female impersonator, a drag artist. Given my biological situation, this was a stupid and unreasonable reaction. My body was wholly female, the proof striking me every time I stared in a mirror or visited the toilet. Alice was no man, and yet...?

"I don't know how." I blurted out to Lorna. "You'll have to show me."

"Alright, love." My unexpected outburst surprised her. "After tea, we'll go up to my room, and I'll explain how. You've obviously forgotten. Do you need to shave your legs?"

I looked at them, and so did she. Fine, downy hairs were showing. Lorna let out a despairing sigh. "We'd better do something about that too.

Unsightly hairs appearing through your stockings are not a good look, and they can become uncomfortable and unsightly. You're going to have to start shaving your legs."

Edie and I took turns washing up and drying after tea. Today it was my turn to wash and hers to dry. As soon as we finished, Lorna called me upstairs, adding, "You better come along too, Edie, and save me showing how to do this twice."

The one thing I knew was how to shave. Shaving my legs smooth was new and different from shaving my face. For one thing, there was more to shave. For another, it was young skin and tender. Edie watched, entranced, and then happened to mention someone's sister shaving her underarms. Shaving underarms? Silently I groaned at the thought. Lorna said we would leave underarms for another time. So began the whole business of how to deal with suspender belts and stockings.

"Suspender belts need tucking inside your knickers," Lorna explained, "not over them. Otherwise, going to the toilet will become a problem." This had not immediately occurred to me. The reason for feeding the suspender straps through the leg openings now made sense. There was other practical advice. A wider suspender belt was better but needed to fit snugly around the waist. Wider ones sagged less when holding up the stockings.

The nylons were thirty denier, Pretty Polly. Edie wanted to know what denier meant, so Lorna explained. The finer the stocking material, the smaller the denier number. The higher the number, the thicker the nylon and less opaque. Thirty to forty deniers were warmer to wear in winter. The ten-denier stockings were lightweight and sheer. They were the nearest to make your legs look natural during the summer months.

"Don't tell me you didn't know, Edie," I mocked, covering my ignorance by pretending how an older sister would act.

"Bet you didn't either!" She countered.

"Stop it, the pair of you!" Lorna reproached me rather than Edie. Next, she demonstrated how to put on a stocking. "Nylons can ladder easily, so care must be taken putting them on, so never rush. You can do it standing up or sitting down. Either way, you must make sure you can sit or stand after attaching them to the straps. The straps shouldn't pull the stockings too tight when sitting or standing."

Lorna stressed when buying stockings, I needed to make sure to get the right size. The right size was all-important. Stockings bunching around your ankles were not a pretty sight. Too short, and they were a waste of money. She had chosen a size based on my shoe size and height.

As a man, I had never understood the dark arts involved when buying women's nylons. I had more idea about putting stockings on having watched Ivy. To wear nylons was another matter. Lorna told me, putting them on and wearing them came with practice.

I studied the information on the packet. Pretty Polly; seam-free, sized 8½ to 11, Sherry colour. I had to admit the description of the shade was accurate. They were a good fit too. What worried me was how I enjoyed staring at my legs in the mirror. There was no doubt about it. My legs did look amazingly pretty in stockings. There was so much more to learn about female apparel than I had ever envisaged. When it came to clothes, makeup, and fashion, it was a world of its own. Angie had begun my education, but there was so much more I was going to have to learn. Tonight, seeing myself in stockings, I fell in love with how I looked.

To be honest, wearing suspender belts proved a pain and uncomfortable until I found some where the straps didn't dig into my thighs. The whole stockings and suspender thing annoyed me no end in the beginning. I got used to them quicker than I expected. Men may find stockings and suspenders sexy and alluring, but as a woman, I never did. Thank heavens tights came along. So much more practical.

Edie, having watched her mother's demonstration, decided she too wanted to wear stockings. There had been a hint of envy in her eyes as she had looked on. Lorna promised she could have some to wear at weekends, although this was conditional. Edie would have to take good care of the stockings. When she proved she could look after her nylons, she could start wearing them in the Fourth Form.

On my first day at Boots, they confined my duties to checking and filling shelves. My other tasks included making sure the shelves were kept neat and fully stocked. In addition, I had to deal with customers. The worst part of the job was standing all day. If you have never stood behind a shop counter in a narrow aisle, you can have no idea how miserable it can be.

At the end of my first day at Boots, they told me I might be allowed to assist on the cosmetics and perfumes counter. This could only happen after my initiation into the esoteric mysteries of Helena Rubenstein and Yardley. There was far more to cosmetics than I expected, which did come as a surprise. I struggled to look excited at the prospect. One thing I had not reckoned on was on seeing a girl from my school coming in to browse. I was surprised how many came in during the afternoon to look around, some even spending their pocket money. Teenage girls, I already knew, were notorious for their obsession with cosmetics.

I had not mentioned getting a Saturday job to anyone except Angie and Jackie. Neither would have said anything to anyone else, so it could only have been Edie.

Cathy, I knew, had started to hang around Woolworth's cosmetic counter as soon as she turned thirteen. Edie was doing so already. The memory of Ivy becoming annoyed with Cathy for wanting makeup from Woolworths returned. In the end, I had quietly slipped her five shillings to let her buy some Miners. It had made her day.

Luckily the girls from my school who came in were Fourth Formers and a couple in the Fifth. Word would get around on Monday. No doubt next Saturday would prove far more interesting.

Part of my lunch breaks coincided with Angie finishing work. We had agreed to meet up with Cathy at a nearby coffee bar. I thought it was about time the two of them should meet. My daughter had always been a quiet child. Hardly surprising, given how vocal and bossy Ivy could be. The two appeared to get on, which pleased me. I hoped Cathy could also make a friendship with Angie, and perhaps it would help to bring my daughter out of herself.

After Angie left to go shopping, I slipped Cathy a lipstick I had bought as a present. Cathy protested, saying she could not accept the gift. Quietly she reminded me I was no longer able to keep helping her. I had to stop trying to be her father and become her friend instead. Even though she spoke in her softest voice, I had to smile. A pensioner sitting at an adjacent table glanced in our direction. His puzzled face, letting us know he wondered if he had misheard her words.

The rest of my first day at work passed quickly. When the doors closed, I couldn't wait to rush home. My legs ached from standing for so long, something I had not expected.

Late autumn has never been a favourite time of the year, winter even less. The season had always struck me as grey, damp, and depressing. Summer sunshine and warm weather had made me feel alive when I was Phil Manley. As Alice Liddell, nothing had changed. Winter remained a depressing prospect. Most of all, I detested the cold drizzle with its strong wintery hint of snow as I made my way to Crossfield's bus station. The thought of another winter like the one we experienced in 1963 made me shudder. Lorna had loaned me the use of her umbrella, and I was glad of the protection it offered.

While waiting in the bus shelter, I became aware of being ogled.

As a man and as a young man, I had done my fair share of staring at passing women, young and older. Admiring pretty girls was what men did, and I had never given it much more thought. In my experience, men are rarely aware of anyone looking them over. At least, in my experience as a man and as a boy. I could not remember any girl ever giving me the eye until I had turned nineteen. This evening, waiting in the bus station shelter, I noticed men openly eyeing me, staring at my legs. Whether it was the man in the young woman or the woman in me, I was unsure. Whichever it was, the sensation left me unnerved and uncomfortable.

In those fleeting moments, I realised for the first time, women were always on display. I was going to be stared at by men, whether I liked it or not. As a man, this was something I had never thought about, and now as Alice, not until this evening. It was the way it was. Like Alice, I would have to start getting used to men looking at me.

The relief I felt when a middle-aged woman sat down next to me was indescribable.

Chapter 14

The Human Jungle – John Barry 7 & Orchestra (Columbia DB7003 – 1963)

Monday 21 November 1966

Dr. Piller and I did share something in common. An interest in identity. Mine. She admitted identity issues were her specialism. It fascinated me too, for not dissimilar reasons. The good doctor wanted to see if I had gone through a personal identity crisis since leaving the hospital.

Click. The tape recorder began recording my responses once more.

How was I coping with my amnesia? Were any more of my memories returning? Was the absence of personal memories creating any problems? Was I unsure of who I was? Did I even know myself? In other words, was I experiencing an identity crisis? The truth? Yes, I was, although not the one Dr. Piller was investigating. Mine was not one I could ever admit to having.

The doctor continued with her explanation. Everyone defined their identity, the self, as those memories that made up who they were. An identity crisis occurred when someone did not, or could not, remember those memories. Dr. Piller insisted my loss of memories constituted an identity crisis.

I had an identity crisis, alright. My now self was unsure of myself now. Though not because of my feigned amnesia. Amnesia was an excuse, something I had concocted on the spot. No, my issue was understanding what I was as well as whom. Was I a soul imprisoned in another body? Or was I an assorted collection of memories plunged into a dying girl's brain? And if I was neither one nor the other, then who or what was I? Of course, there was an even more obvious question to which I had no answer. How had I come to be in Alice's body?

During the appointment, I struggled to keep my irritable mood under control. My breasts felt sore. For the last day or two, I had experienced worrying headaches. Headaches had been something I had rarely if ever suffered as a man. I didn't feel too pleased to be here with Dr. Piller. Nor was mood improved listening in discomfort to what she had to say.

According to the good doctor, I suffered from a condition she diagnosed as a generalised rather than dissociative amnesia. The doctor said it was a

70

possibility my brief death and subsequent resuscitation had wiped my memory. What puzzled the doctor most were the changes Lorna had observed in me and had let her know. I went cold as I listened. Lorna had told Piller my personality had altered completely. So had my mannerisms and even my handwriting. I had not expected Lorna to have pointed these out to the psychiatrist. Yet she had, and in considerable detail. There was more. Horrified, I listened further to what Lorna had told her and froze.

Dr. Piller now suggested a course of treatment. I seethed in silence, trying not to let anger get the better of me. She wanted to try hypnosis to restore my memories and my old self. I had no intention of allowing her to go prying in my unconscious. Too much was at stake. For several seconds I imagine being trapped in an episode of the TV series *The Human Jungle*. Except Piller radiated far more of a threat than Herbert Lom ever had as Doctor Corder.

"Your case interests me. It seems your episodic memory is largely, and probably, temporarily lost, though your semantic and implicit memory functions quite well."

I hadn't a clue what she was on about. So, I asked her to explain. Which I suppose anyone would do, especially a confused teenage girl.

Episodic memory housed long-term memories. Remembrances like your first day at school, being at a friend's birthday party, or going to a fairground. Implicit memory was an unconscious memory, such as knowing how to swim. Once learned, an implicit memory became imprinted permanently and was automatically remembered without thought whenever needed. The gist of what she explained seemed clear enough.

And as for the hypnosis? I was never going to let it happen under any circumstances.

"I'm quite happy the way I am," I began. "Some of my memories have returned. I'm sure the rest will resurface in due course. *It's no use going back to yesterday because I was a different person then,* and I've changed even more since. You can forget the hypnosis. I don't need anyone prying in my head."

If I thought the slap to her professionalism would be the end of it, I was mistaken. Katie Piller had no intention of giving up on hypnotism.

"A mind without memory is a mind with no objective existence. What is the self without its memories?" The psychiatrist posed the question and paused. "Your mind, without all of its memory intact, is incomplete. Hypnosis is the key to unlocking your mind to release those missing memories locked away in your unconscious. You need your lost memories restoring."

"No, thank you, Dr. Piller. My lost memories will return without you tampering inside my head. They'll come back in their own good time. I'm sorry, but I don't believe I need further treatment. There is nothing wrong with me. So, I won't be attending any more of your sessions."

The doctor became quite huffy and insistent. My determined refusal to be hypnotised and to have no further treatment were not well received. There was more than a hint of menace in her softly spoken words. "We shall see what your mother has to say about your decision."

"It doesn't matter what she says. I will not be coming back."

My first real fallout with Lorna followed.

Whether my obstinacy caused the argument or hers, I was unsure. Probably Lorna did not want to upset an old school friend. In the end, we reached a compromise. I would continue to attend sessions, but hypnosis would be out of the question. Admittedly, we would not have reached this compromise without haggling over my going to the party. If I wanted to go to the party, I had to keep attending Dr. Piller's sessions. My sympathies for Lorna ran deep. More than I imagined. Even though I had to continue going, at the same time, I didn't need or want to start an unnecessary row. The important thing was to keep our home life happy and for me to remain a dutiful and loving daughter.

Terry Hare might have the answers I was desperately seeking. Aside from which another side of my curiosity needed satisfying. What attraction had Alice had for him if any? Would I feel the same as she had? More and more, I understood how much my body guided my responses.

Period cramps were things I had never experienced since finding myself in a woman's body. Alice's periods had begun at fourteen and were irregular and light, seldom lasting a day or two, or so Lorna told me. What I experienced later in the evening at home after seeing Dr. Piller was agonising. It left me doubled up on the living room floor in front of the gas fire. The pain was excruciating. It was as though my lower abdomen was being crushed from the inside. As a man, I had experienced stomach aches and indigestion, but this was nothing comparable. Not even close.

"What's the matter with you?" Edie tapped me with her toe end.

"I'm in agony!" I screeched.

"Mum!" Edie shouted.

Of course, I ought to have known what the problem was. Edie helped me upstairs to our bedroom. Lorna came up ten minutes later with a hot water bottle, some Aspro, and a sanitary towel. All those male jokes about the time of the month and strange behaviour were no longer amusing. Period pain was an extremely unpleasant downside to being a woman. Was I going to have to face this for the next thirty and more years every month?

Chapter 15

So What? – Bill Black Combo (London HLU 9594 – 1962)

Saturday, 26 November 1967

Lorna was scandalised when she saw the dress Angie had loaned me for the party. On Angie, the hemline was more than a good couple of inches above the knee. On me, it was more.

"You can't possibly wear this dress! The hem is too far above your knee!" She exclaimed in horror.

"For heaven's sake, mum! It's only showing some of my thighs and knees! Nothing else!"

Angie had insisted I borrowed one of her dresses after seeing what was in my wardrobe.

"Oh, no!" Angie had exclaimed. "You have absolutely nothing in there. I'm going to lend you one of mine, Alice. I can't have my friend going to a party dressed like an overgrown twelve-year-old, or a middle-aged woman."

Angie was like any young teenage woman, keen to wear the latest fashions. Bill Thornton was a generous father. No wonder she always looked like an aspiring model. I became the beneficiary of her wardrobe emptying. That was how I came by a sleeveless turquoise blue shift cocktail dress with a lacy round collar. I performed a twirl and admired my appearance in the mirror. Then, in a single brief instance I understood how female I had become.

There was no longer any reaction to seeing myself as Alice. I'd become accustomed to my face and looks. Finally, I accepted myself. Each new day I was increasingly more and more a young woman and less and less who I had once been. My acceptance of myself as Alice felt complete. Even behaving like a woman had become second nature as I had settled into this new life. I found it natural, almost instinctive, to twirl and check my dress and myself in the mirror. What remained of my sense of masculinity was deserting me as each day passed. Soon there would be nothing left, only faded memories of who I had once been. I was young once more, and I was in love with life. Something I could never recall experiencing as a young man at the same age.

Lorna wasn't happy about my going to a party hosted by someone we didn't know. Reluctantly she let me go knowing I would be with Jackie and three other girls from my form. If she had known what kind of party we were going to, she would probably have tried to stop me. In all honesty, even I was clueless about what to expect. Was I in for a surprise! Brenda and Pamela had a pretty good idea, and I ought to have guessed. On the way, I called for Jackie, who was as excited as I had ever seen her.

Jackie's mother had made her a sheath dress from a Vogue pattern. She looked strikingly sophisticated and grown up in her satiny dark brown patterned dress. Jackie was also wearing expensive new-fangled glitter tights and patent leather shoes with kitten heels. The acne on her chin had been expertly masked. The butterfly spectacles had gone, replaced by an elegant cat-eye frame. Tonight, Jackie's transformation was complete, and it was also a new beginning. She would remain a changed girl long after tonight was over.

We met up with Pamela and Marjorie at their homes on Saville Park Road and set off. It was a fifteen-minute walk to Kensington Road. I have to admit we were in an excitable and giddy state as we walked there. Pamela and Marjorie had each downed a couple of large Sherries in secret before leaving their respective homes. Brenda knew exactly where the party was being held and led the way chattering incessantly with excitement.

Sam the Sham and The Pharaohs *Wooly Bully* was playing when we arrived at the large, impressive terrace house. The sound of the music escaping through the front door to greet our arrival sent a genuine thrill through me.

The house was a beautifully appointed home with tasteful wallpaper to match the carpets. When we entered, it became clear boys outnumbered girls three to one. Someone directed us to a bedroom at the top of the first landing, where we could leave our coats on a double bed, along with all the other coats. More teenagers kept arriving as we made our way back downstairs. The only part of the house brightly lit was the kitchen. A partially blacked-out standard lamp ensured the lounge remained dark. The living room opposite had a single table lamp for illumination. The light allowed three youths to keep choosing and playing records. On came the sound of The Troggs *With A Girl Like You* as we walked in the room The same three youths never left the record player all evening except to get an occasional drink.

There were other girls here. Brenda identified some of them as Sixth Formers from Princess Mary's Grammar as we circulated. They didn't seem too friendly, staring dagger-eyed in our direction. We were competition. Not that I particularly cared. My sole interest in coming was to meet Terry Hare. Gently, I pulled Brenda away from the boys by the record player. Which one was Terry, and where was he? We found him moments later, chatting in the kitchen to two girls, one of whom I recognised from our Sixth Form.

With a Double Diamond beer bottle in one hand and an almost smoked cigarette in the other, he was nothing like I had imagined. How disappointing, I thought. Surely Alice must have had a better taste in boys? Terry Hare reminded me of the actor who had played Flashman in *Tom Brown's Schooldays*. Hardly a recommendation with his almost identical beaky nose.

"How nice to see you again, Alice. I didn't realise you'd lost your memory until Brenda told me." He looked uneasily at Brenda. This immediately put me on my guard.

"Is the rumour true you died in hospital, and they revived you?" Asked the girl from the other school.

"Penny," she referred back to her, "has been telling me all about you."

"Has she indeed? What *have* you been saying, *Penny*?" The thin-lipped blonde with the flipped hairstyle gave me an awkward glance as I turned to Terry Hare. "The truth is the doctor pronounced me dead. It seems I was dead for forty minutes before they wheeled me off to the mortuary. On the way there, I came too and sat up. I don't think I've ever seen anyone so scared."

"You were d-dead for f-f-forty minutes," the girl stuttered, horrified, in disbelief. "You are joking?"

"No. No joke. It's true. I did die. Then I rose from the dead. Scary, eh? You don't shake hands with the devil and say you're joking." There was genuine fear on her face as I spoke the last words. She made the Catholic sign of the cross. Her anguished expression nearly set me off giggling. I teased her a little more. Lowering my voice, I uttered darkly, "Am I scaring you?"

Of course, I had no intention of providing the true explanation surrounding my miraculous revival. I'd not been dead for that length of time, but I enjoyed the exaggeration.

Terry Hare frowned, staring at me quizzically, trying to take in what I'd said. "You were clinically dead? Technically dead?"

"Yes. You were there when I collapsed, weren't you? That's what the girls told me. I want to know what happened."

76

He exchanged glances with Penny, who continued to look aghast. Then he came closer to me, stubbing out his cigarette in an ashtray. Placing a hand on my shoulder, the smell of beer and cigarettes on his breath, he whispered we should go into the hallway. What he wanted to tell me was private. Intrigued by his suggestion, I agreed.

Out in the hallway, I found myself with my back to the wall. Terry Hare had pinned me against it leaning over me. His arm was above me, resting against the wall. He had me physically contained.

"You don't remember collapsing?"

"No. Not a thing. Not even passing out. Everything that happened in my life before I died has gone."

He began recounting in whispered tones what had taken place. We'd been walking in the park. I had looked pale and tired but not unwell. In any case, I was not my usual self, complaining of an awful headache. His words implied he and Alice had met before. Had he been her boyfriend?

Something about his nervousness made me suspicious. This couldn't be true. I couldn't think why, but my senses seemed to confirm my suspicion. I genuinely could not imagine Alice falling for him. The suffocating way he now had me backed against the wall wasn't pleasant either. His breath reeked the closer he came to me. The nasty mix of beer, cigarettes, and what smelled like polo mints made my stomach churn. Close up, I could see the blackheads and spots on his face, which didn't improve matters. I felt myself squirm. Honestly, Alice? I could not believe she had fancied him.

He continued his account of the events. Alice had fainted outside the public library as they were about to go in, which was fortunate. The library had a telephone, and it was there they had made a call for an ambulance when she became unresponsive. The ambulance men had arrived and taken her away. There was not much more he could tell me.

As he finished talking, he made a move to kiss me. I jumped out from under him, letting him almost kiss the wall behind me instead. It looked so comical I couldn't help smirking. Terry Hare looked annoyed and began claiming we had started going out together. I was supposed to be his girlfriend. His story didn't ring true, nor his claim that I had been his girlfriend. Maybe Alice had been his girlfriend, but I doubted it. Not if my bodily responses had anything to say about it.

"It's no use harking back, Terry, because I was a different girl then. And I'm a very different girl now," I pouted and mocked, as I walked away. How I came out with this line surprised me. How appropriate it felt when The

Spencer Davis Group's *Somebody Help Me* came to an end, followed swiftly by The Rolling Stones *(I Can't Get No) Satisfaction*.

"Why don't you chat up, Penny."

"She's my cousin," he snarled back, 'that would be inappropriate."

Our group had split up. When I went into the living room, Brenda rushed up to me, wanting to know what had happened. She kept staring nervously through the door as I told her.

"I'll go and chat him up if you don't want him." Off she disappeared, leaving me in the middle of the room open-mouthed. I couldn't help grinning, imagining Brenda jumping in to become my substitute.

From the corner of my eye, I spied Jackie. Some boy was chatting to her in the corner. Marjorie was likewise preoccupied. I was suddenly on my own and thinking, good luck with him, Brenda.

There was no sign of Pamela. Penny came in with her friend Lynn and persuaded me to join them dancing in the middle of the room in a tight little circle. I had learned the dance steps in a lunch hour at school. We spent a good while dancing around our handbags, chatting, and laughing. All the time we danced, we loved suggestively teasing the boys looking at us. When we were tired, Penny and Lynn dragged me off to the kitchen. There we managed to find a half-full bottle of Ben Shaw's Dandelion and Burdock. Nothing alcoholic was left, which was just as well. I had no intention of restarting drinking. Alcohol had contributed to killing me in my other life.

One of the many things I appreciated finding myself as Alice was how keen all my senses were. Being young again was so much more of a sensuous and pleasurable experience. It left me with a constant feeling of elation. My smoking, drinking, and bad eating habits had been the death of me as an adult. These same vices had also ruined my sense of taste and smell. My eyesight had also begun to deteriorate in my forties. A year or so before my death I'd had to start wearing spectacles for reading. Nor had my hearing been as good as when I had been a young man. I put the poor hearing down to the effects of explosions and artillery fire during the war. No wonder music sounded so much better, more defined, and colourful. And as for my sense of touch? My tactile perception was so considerably more sensitive. Fabrics and materials felt far softer or coarser than I remembered, depending on what I touched. I found myself so much more touchy-feely and responsive than I could ever remember. My senses were alive and a pleasurable joy I no longer took for granted. Even sipping warm dandelion and burdock proved my taste buds were better now.

Penny and Lynn proved good company, making me feel welcome. Our conversation proved interesting. In whispers, they informed me, boys, on their own, generally found it hard approaching a group of three or more girls. As a third girl, it was a means of keeping young men at bay. Usually, most were too intimidated to approach. Penny explained as Terry's cousin, she had come reluctantly. She had dragged her equally reluctant friend along as company. They were interested in knowing what it was like to suffer from amnesia. My explanation was simple, if untruthful. I had to live with what I learned about myself from others. In its own way, I supposed it was a truthful explanation.

When I voiced my uncertainty about Terry being my boyfriend, Penny and her friend giggled. Terry, she told me in a whisper, was always trying to chat up girls. So, far he had not got very far to her knowledge. Besides, she remembered me. I was shy and very self-conscious. On the school grapevine, girls were remarking about how very different I had become since returning from the hospital. I looked at the clock and groaned. The time had flown, and it was now ten past ten. The time to round up the others had arrived, and, like Cinderella, the time to leave had come. I began the round-up.

Jackie was still in the living room talking to the same boy. Marjorie was sitting on some boy's lap, trying to suck his lips from his face. The others were nowhere around. I decided to retrieve our coats from the bedroom. As I dashed up the stairs, an intoxicated youth attempted to fondle my behind. My annoyed glare had little effect. I had to slap his hands away twice. The bedroom was in darkness when I entered and fumbled for the light switch. The muffled gasping sound of a girl's breathing came from under a shuffling pile of coats as the light came on.

On removing the coats, I found Pamela under them all. She was not alone. Talk about being compromised. There she was, passionately kissing some boy, her dress up around her waist, his fingers inside her pink lace knickers. The action froze. I had no time to think, so I blurted out, it was time for us to be going. Pamela's petrified face remains with me even now, years later. It was the most comical mix of, caught in the headlights, open-mouthed near orgasm, mixed with panic, embarrassment, and fear.

"I'll meet you downstairs," I mumbled apologetically, "come when you're ready."

I swear I said it unintentionally, and it was not how I intended it to sound.

There was another snog fest going on in the next bedroom, but no sign of Brenda. Someone suggested trying the attic bedroom up another flight of stairs. I finally found Brenda alright. With Terry Hare. This proved even more highly embarrassing. I should have blushed. Instead, I burst out laughing, which was infinitely worse. Slamming the door behind me, I ran down the stairs with the coats sniggering as I did so. Somehow, I doubted I would ever forget seeing them kissing while Brenda masturbated him.

A few minutes later, I had to whisper in Brenda's ear, "When you get home, I should try to clean the stain off your dress before your mum sees it. Beetroot faced and abashed, Brenda wrapped her coat tightly around herself. Pamela was equally upset. On our walk back, she begged me in whispers not to tell anyone what I had seen. I did not want to distress her further, but the boy in question would most likely be bragging about it right now. I could imagine him saying to his mates something like, here, have a sniff of Pamela. Having been a male, that kind of juvenile bragging was, unfortunately, all too likely.

Brenda said nothing. Her awkwardness wanted to make me smile, but I didn't want to increase her embarrassed uneasiness. Not that I would ever blackmail her. I could, with a News of the World-style revelations. I would leave that to Terry Hare. No doubt he would be crowing about it already. I decided to put her mind at rest. So, in whispers, I told her I would never say a word about her popping his cork. That made her giggle, as did my little singsong with changed lyrics. *You had his whole world in your hands; you got his little bitty dicky in your hands.*

Unlike Pamela and Brenda, Marjorie was full of it. There was no stopping her bragging how hard his cock had felt against her when she was snogging him. Jackie and I found ourselves laughing aloud, not even noticing the cold and dampness as we linked arms and walked home. We laughed even harder, joking about how hard Marjorie had tried to suction the skin off the boy's lips. She could not stop boasting about what an expert kisser he was. Marjorie had arranged to meet him next Saturday night. He said they could go to Palin's dancing. Jackie and I left the other girls as we walked on to our homes. Jackie was breezy and happier than I had ever seen her.

"I have a date! Ian wants me to meet him after school on Monday," She announced proudly.

"And you got to kiss him too, didn't you?"

"I did." Jackie beamed and performed a twirl on the pavement. "I did, didn't I?"

Had I understood how randy teenage girls of sixteen and seventeen were, I would have had a much more exciting time as a young man.

80

Five minutes late. I expected a few reprimanding words from Lorna. She glanced up at the clock on the mantelpiece and gave me a look as if to say ten thirty-five was not ten-thirty. "Did you have a good time, dear?"

"Yes, we did. I got to know a girl from our Sixth Form called Penny and her friend, Lynn. We had a good natter and danced."

"And boys?"

"Spotty smokers, trying to be men and not doing a good job of it." My description made her smile. I grinned and detected a silent sigh of relief as I spoke.

Tucked up in bed, I could not get over what I had seen Pamela and Brenda doing. As a boy and a man, I had masturbated. Most boys and men did, to dampen down the urges when there was no outlet. Since finding myself as a teenage girl, I had resisted the temptation. Tonight, I tried and learned something I had never suspected. Female orgasm was more intense and longer-lasting than anything a man could experience.

Chapter 16

The Thoughts of Emerlist Davjack (Immediate IM059 – 1967)

Thursday 3, December 1967

There was the knowledge I had acquired in my life as Phil Manley, and there was the knowledge I was adding as Alice Liddell. General Studies was either a relief or a distraction for the girls in my group. The lesson on comparative religions struck home when Buddhism and reincarnation received a mention. Not so much the talk of Buddhism as of reincarnation. At some point, I reasoned, I might have the courage to start asking myself the how or the why of it in my case.

I knew nothing about reincarnation. Unfortunately, neither did the girls in the class. When Pamela asked the teacher to explain, this instantly gripped my interest. The school library contained a little more information, though not enough to satisfy my need for more. The following day I went to the local library on Skircoat Green Road, where Alice had collapsed. The librarian remembered me and enquired about my health before suggesting I try the library in town. The reference section would have what I was searching for, so I went the following day.

It stood to reason that if we had a soul, we needed a body to house it. Without a body, the soul would be incapable of a separate existence. Buddhist belief suggested that when we died, if we had not achieved a state of spiritual perfection, then we would be reborn once more. Or rather, our mind would be reborn in a new body. We would become an infant once again. We would be destined to lead another earthly life as someone else, somewhere else. In this next life, our mind would have no recollection of our previous life. At the end of each life, we would progress on to the next. We would continue these constant rebirths until our souls reached enlightenment. A state of nirvana, whatever that was supposed to be. So, why did I recall my previous life in such detail? Yet why had I no recollection of my life before that one? Or the life before that, and so on?

The other question bothering me had to do with wondering if the mind and soul were the same? If they were not, did this explain why previous life recollections were rare? This was what the books I had read said. So, did memories imprinted on the brain remain with the body after death? If they did, did the soul or mind move on unencumbered by the memories? In which case, why had all my memories transferred to Alice's brain?

If a soul travelled on without personal memories, then by rights, so should mine. I should have had no recollection of my past life. Also, according to what I read in the town library, previous lives recalled tended to reappear a lifetime later. Usually, these came from children who remembered and spoke about their memories of a recent previous life. None of what I read applied to me. My reincarnation, if it was indeed a reincarnation, must have been instantaneous. Nowhere could I find any mention of anything like the instant re-housing in the adolescent body of the opposite sex.

My death certificate, if I had had one, would have recorded my time of death. Frank, I supposed, could confirm my return to life as Alice. He would remember to within a few minutes when I had revived. This instant transfer had me thinking. My past life was no illusion. I had lived it; I remembered it vividly and in detail, though in this life, it had begun to take on a dreamlike quality.

What I understood about the self ruled out the idea it was illusory. There was more to the self than the brain because mine was dead, buried, and decomposing in a grave. If I had a soul, then it might explain how I survived my death. It could also explain how my unique identity had survived and now lived on in someone else's body. What other rational explanation could there be?

Supernatural, or divine intervention of some kind, could not be ruled out. Although I had never been a true believer, I couldn't readily dismiss the idea after what had happened. After all, how else could I have found myself alive and in Alice's body if not with the assistance of some supernatural or preternatural force? All I could do for the present was make the best of my situation, as I had no answers. Whatever, or whoever, had given me this second chance to live remained a mystery. Maybe sooner, maybe later, the answer might be revealed. Then again, I might never learn the truth.

The gift of a new life remained a gift. I had to treasure this life. In time, I would come to realise my new life had a purpose and a mission. I would come to understand why I had a destiny to live as a woman.

For the present, I needed to leave my conjectures aside. My life as Alice had one immediate purpose. First and foremost, my duty remained to help my new family. Lorna, Edie, and Frank had become my number one priority, along with Cathy. As soon as I could, I would earn money to support and help them. To do this would mean obtaining good qualifications so I could get a high-earning career. I made a promise to myself once more to do that. Which did not mean I should not begin to enjoy my life as Alice.

At eighteen, I had enlisted, and as a soldier, there had been no time and no opportunity to enjoy my youth. The war had torn my youth from me. In my new life as Alice, I vowed this life would be different.

Chapter 17

Girl Talk – Tony Bennett
From The Movie Song Album (CBS UK LP SBPG 62677 1966)

Friday 2, December 1967

Angie was lucky to have a three-quarter bed. So soft and so comfortable, I envied her its luxury. I wished I had a bed like it. My single three-foot-wide bed was almost as hard and as uncomfortable as the bunk I'd had in the army. Laid on the bed, talking to one another from opposite ends, we relaxed, sipping mugs of hot chocolate. Angie was a whole learning experience for me. Here was a young woman who made me feel at ease and comfortable in myself. In her company, I could relate to what it meant to be female. My new life no longer felt bizarre. During our sleepover, I finally gave up any lingering pretensions to manhood.

Women and girls who got on with one another loved each other's company in a different way to men. As a man, the conversation had rarely, if ever, involved anything of an emotional nature. In my experience, men talked about things or activities. Personal and emotional topics were not seen as masculine. Women talked far more freely.

Girl talk had become second nature for me, almost routine. It had started as a means of establishing my female credentials and identity. Without even realising it, girl talk had stealthily assimilated me into my new gender. Without it, I could never have bonded with other girls. It had become a completely normal activity, as had the topics of conversation.

Hair became our first topic of conversation. Angie complimented my recent Mod-style bob cut and its beautiful silky condition. As a man, I had never understood the importance of hair and hair maintenance to women. Why it was so necessary to visit a hairdresser often. Ivy never explained, only insisted on going to have her hair done. Now I finally and fully appreciated why our hair was fundamental to our self-image and pride.

I took pride in my gorgeous head of thick, soft, and luxuriant, honey-coloured hair. I had begun to enjoy brushing it to perfection and looking at it in the mirror. We discussed the merits of the different shampoos and conditioners we used, moving on to which hairstylists in town were the best. I would need to keep going regularly, now I'd had mine styled.

Cosmetics came next, followed by looking at the latest fashions in magazines. Inevitably our conversation turned to talk about family and friends, then to boys. There was brief talk about news items but none about politics. Clothes, yes, makeup, yes, people, yes, politics, no. The nearest to talking about politics was wondering if we would ever go on a CND march or carry a ban the bomb placard.

Tonight, we were comfortable and happy in our own company. Here and now, I was at peace with who I had become. There was a brief lull as we savoured the hot chocolate drink in slow sips. Then Angie asked the question that started me pondering my sexuality.

"Can you remember if you are a virgin?"

For a moment, I wondered if I had misheard? My expression made her giggle.

"I'm pretty sure I must be," I replied, "at least to the best of my knowledge."

The question did not embarrass me, but it gave way to an unexpected question in return. "What was it like... your first time? Did it hurt?"

Angie looked up at the ceiling for a few seconds. "Too much is made of it, Alice. It's overrated and something you have to go through, one of life's experiences. Honestly, I wondered what the fuss was all about after it happened. Take it from me, it's nothing like the way they write about it in the romances. It's sweaty and messy, and it hurts. At least, I found it painful. After the first time, it gradually hurt less and less. Why do you ask? Are you planning to lose yours?"

"Goodness, no. Not at the moment!" I protested, hearing the astonishment in my voice. "I am definitely not ready to do it."

Angie stared at me quizzically for several seconds. With her head tilted to one side, she asked hesitantly. "Do you fancy girls rather than boys?"

"Noooo!" I expanded, shaking my head. Did I, I questioned myself? When I'd been Phil, yes. Did I still find girls attractive? The strange thing was I had no sexual inclination towards girls or women any longer. Young men? I was afraid to ask myself. I'd never inclined towards men. This, I suppose, was the problem. My mind was saying no, but my body was starting to tell me something else.

"So, have you met any boys you like the look of?" She pressed.

I shook my head. "None, I fancy."

What else could I say? I was changing. I had changed. Much of my maleness had evaporated into insignificance. I had been a prisoner of my

86

body as Phil Manley. My maleness had shaped my old life. Now I was a prisoner of Alice Liddell's body but with limited experience of life as a woman. If my fate was to live in a female body, what else could I ever hope to be but female. I retained my memories of my life as a man, but that was all they were. My female body was another matter. It had already begun to change and affect my mind and my personality. I was undergoing a metamorphosis of another kind.

Years later, I would learn and understand how female hormones and the female brain operated differently from the male. For now, I was deep into finally accepting my new gender.

"So, what attracts you to a boy?" I asked, changing the conversation.

Angie swept her hair back over her ear and began to play pensively with an earring, "I thought I knew until I met Mack."

"How?"

"Okay," Angie began, "every time I see him, it's the way he is with me. His smile, his eyes, the way he looks at me. Such gorgeous hazel eyes. Oh, and that voice of his! It lulls me into a happy, dreamy state. And it's the way he listens to me when we talk. I mean, he really listens and takes an interest in me as a person. I get shivers when we talk. Then, I can't forget the tenderness after we made love. Even now, he never avoids me or acts all embarrassed by what happened. He's so grown up for his age. Mack has such a lovely sense of humour, he makes me smile and laugh, and it's not dirty innuendos like his cousin Tom. For me, a man would have to respect me and never abuse me as the two other bastards did."

The mention of those men tripped an awful momentary darkness in her eyes.

The smile returned, and I knew she was still smitten by this young man. After all these months, he still filled her thoughts, her dreams, and maybe her fantasies.

"You need to start going out and enjoying life. Why don't you come out with the girls and me? Why don't you come dancing with us? You can meet Mack and Effy, his girlfriend. She's lovely, and we have become really good friends, would you believe? You'd like her and Mack."

"Where? When?"

"The Jazz Club, downtown. Surely your mum won't mind you going to the club with me and some of my friends? You'd really enjoy it."

"The Jazz Club? Is this the same place you call *The Plebs*? The one you told me about? The Mod place?" I queried.

"Yes, we could have a fab time." Angie livened up at the idea. "You'd have no trouble finding yourself a boyfriend. Afterwards, we could continue with a sleepover."

The idea of going out appealed. Ever since attending the party, I had listened to some of the girls talking about what a great time they'd had going out on Friday and Saturday nights. I wanted to experience the same. Why should I waste my newfound youth on staying in? Why should I not go out and enjoy myself and see what all the fuss and excitement was about?

"It sounds like a great idea. What about next Saturday instead rather than tomorrow?"

Angie's face fell. "Ben E. King's appearing at the Twisted Wheel all-nighter in Manchester. I've already made arrangements to drive over."

"Couldn't I come over with you?"

"I have a full car if Mack and Effy come with me."

"Oh! I see." I must have sounded upset.

"Look, stay over tomorrow, and we can go down the club together. We can go to The Wheel another time. What do you say?"

"Won't your mum mind me staying over another night, Angie?"

"Why should she? We did weekend sleepovers when we were little. She wouldn't have a problem. And anyway, since she's been unwell, the tranquillisers and sleeping pills knock her out for the count. As for dad, he's away overnight most weekends from Friday to Sunday travelling on business with my Uncle Den. My mum rarely leaves her bedroom when my dad's not here. Gill and I usually have the house to ourselves."

"My mum wouldn't let me stay out longer than ten-thirty, but...if I did stay over with you, I could go," I replied, the idea appealing more and more.

So, this was how teenagers hoodwinked their parents. Stay-overs and sleepovers were not something that had happened during my teenage years.

"What should I wear? I don't have a lot in the way of going out dresses," I continued as she slid off the bed towards her bulging wardrobe.

"I've got a dress or two you can have and some I could let you borrow," Angie replied without looking in my direction. "Let's see what might suit you."

And this was how and when Angie began my transformation into a Mod.

Chapter 18

In The Basement – Etta James & Sugar Pie DeSanto (Chess CRS 8034 – 1966)

Saturday 3, December 1967

Angie convinced Lorna to let me stay over at her house after we went down the club. Her persuasiveness was impressive. As I was to learn, she had an incredible talent when it came to convincing others. A skill she would employ to all our benefits in the future to help build our fortunes.

Tonight, after returning home from Boots, I could hardly wait to walk down to Angie's. The thought of going out on a Saturday night made me feel excited, joyous, and liberated. For the first time since becoming Alice, I experienced a real sense of freedom. Freedom to enjoy myself as her.

Angie hadn't warned me we were going to an all-night event, which explained why we didn't set off until after nine-thirty. We arrived in town a few minutes before ten and walked from the bus station to Silver Street. There we took the shortcut down the side of the Vic Lounge pub through Black Swan Passage into George Square.

The scene greeting our arrival revealed parked scooters with smartly dressed young men and women standing around them or talking in small groups by shop windows. They were waiting for the club to open its doors for the all-nigher at 11.35. These were the young people Angie had enthused about. The town's Mods.

Within seconds of arriving, it became clear Angie was not only popular but also highly regarded. Everyone seemed to know her. Some of the younger girls even looked at her in awe, which struck me as amusing Two girls approached us as we walked to a favourite meeting spot. Angie introduced Carol to me, a short blonde in a tight-fitting suede coat. Her other friend, in a navy-blue leather coat, was Linda.

Linda recognised me immediately, having been a pupil at Crossley in the same year. She had known Alice at school but had left at the same time as Angie. The way Linda looked at me sent a shiver through my body. I could tell she hoped for some response. When I didn't appear to know her, I saw the disappointment. Angie reminded Linda of my amnesia. I touched her arm, adding that although I could not remember her, I could not remember anyone, and I was sure we would become good friends again. Linda smiled, accepting my explanation, exchanging glances with Angie. I learned later we had not been friends at school.

"Where's lover boy?" Angie asked the girl she had introduced as Carol.

"Tom's gone off somewhere with Mack. His cousin is fixing someone's scooter. They'll be late. Tom says Mack will need to clean up before coming out. He said he'd me meet down at the club, the cheapskate."

I could not help noticing the size of Carol's heaving bosom as she spoke. It seemed to want to burst out of her tightly fastened suede coat. Neither could I ignore the reaction in Angie's eyes as she heard the news about Mack. She quickly concealed her disappointment. As we stood talking, we were met by another one of her friends, who Angie introduced as Alan.

To kill some time before going down to the club, we went into the Vic Lounge. We would stay there until kicking out time, which would be half an hour after the last orders bell. Angie slipped Alan a ten-shilling note to get the drinks for the girls and a pint for himself. She reminded him to give her the change.

Clouds of cigarette smoke made my eyes water as we waited for the drinks. I could even taste it in the air each time I drew a breath. There was no chance of me restarting the habit either, not after this reminder.

I had never frequented the Vic Lounge as my old self. The pub had a reputation as a young men's pub. As a middle-aged man, I could see why I had avoided it for a reason. As a young woman, I saw it with different eyes and heard the music with different ears. The jukebox was loud, and the bar was crammed with young men drinking preventing access to it for orders. While Alan and Angie fought their way through to get our drinks, I chatted with the others.

The young men in the Vic seemed more intent on listening to the music and drinking beer rather than chatting up the girls. Some of the records playing on the jukebox I recognised as the Motown ones Angie loved. Others had a grittier sound. As each new record played, Linda kept me informed. This one was by Sam and Dave, that one by Otis Redding, Wilson Pickett, The Impressions, and so on. The music and the sound of the beer glasses clinking made me heady and elated.

When we got our drinks, I felt like the odd one out with my tonic water. The other girls were drinking barley wines. There was nothing wine-like about barley wines. The drink was a strong beer with a high alcohol content guaranteed to quickly make a girl tipsy.

A roar went up as the jukebox played a new song. We began to shuffle to the music where we stood. Nor were we the only ones. Quite a few others in the bar did the same. The urge to dance to the music seemed instinctive. Linda and Angie joined in, chanting *You don't know like I know* in time to the lyrics.

"Love this Sam and Dave single," Linda eagerly announced before continuing to singalong on with the others. We left a few minutes before eleven and stood chatting for a quarter of an hour in the Square. Carol said she would wait with Alan until Tom and Mack turned up on their scooters.

The walk to the club in Cheapside from the Vic took a couple of minutes and no more. A queue had already formed. Fortunately, it was a dry, cold, crisp night, as we stood chatting, shivering, and waited for the doors to open.

I had passed the club countless times on my way to the Upper George at the end of the yard. The pub had been a favourite watering hole of mine. A place where I had supped many a pint, including my last. The pub's lights shone invitingly across the yard's darkness before being extinguished just before the club doors opened. If, as Phil Manley, I'd had to choose a place to die, I supposed the pub would have been as good as anywhere. As it happened, I'd had my wish granted.

Located in what had once been a wholesaler's warehouse, *The Plebs* began life as a Jazz Club. The club's first incarnation had been in mill premises on Pellon Lane. Vandalism had led to its closure and a restart here in the Upper George Yard. These new premises, from what I could remember, had belonged to a fruit and vegetable wholesaler. They had ceased trading years ago and had rented out the basement to the club's owner. Since its reopening, the club had changed over time from a jazz venue to a Mod club. The Plebeians still retained its original name and was often referred to as the Jazz Club. Now older Mod teenagers came to dance to Soul music and to see groups down in the basement.

Entry to the underground premises was by a few steps illuminated by a dingy red light. An ink stamp was applied to your hand as you paid and entered. This pass allowed you to go out and return. A corridor led to the dance floor with toilets and a cloakroom off to the left. The Supremes *You Keep Me Hanging On* came to an end as we took our tickets from the cloakroom attendant. The dance area had already begun to fill with dancers, mainly girls. I recognised, *A Little Piece of Leather* by someone called Donnie Elbert as it started playing.

The air soon became hot and sticky from all the bodies. We took a break and went into the crowded toilets to check makeup and hair before venturing back out into the increasingly steamy atmosphere. As we returned to the dancing, the DJ played Wilson Pickett's *In The Midnight Hour*. Angie showed me the time on her wristwatch. It was midnight. We squeezed into a space, formed another circle, and began to dance around our handbags. The Four Tops *Reach Out And I'll Be There* came next without a pause. These were records I'd heard at Angie's. They were in her collection.

The loudness of the music drowned out any chance of conversation. Not that it mattered. We were here to dance and enjoy ourselves. Talking we could do another time. Stopping out until the early hours and dancing was fun. I didn't know too many of the records played, but the catchy songs and melodies had me. One record was especially catchy: *The Clapping Song*. This had all the girls joining in with the words. Some guys dancing in the next circle made me laugh using alternative lyrics. Instead of *rubber dolly*, they sang rubber johnny as loud as they could.

Angie had schooled me about dance etiquette such as existed. The guys circled in twos and threes, checking out the talent from around the edges of the dance area. Usually, the bravest would approach the girl they fancied. He would ask to join the circle to dance. If they were given the okay, then the other one or two would then follow. After a record or two, they would try chatting to their chosen target between record changes. Naturally, we girls would have the chance to weigh up if any of them were a prospect. If we didn't fancy them, we would give them flat disinterested verbal responses.

Then it could become a little more complicated. We girls had to decide if we found him attractive enough to carry on dancing and chatting. Or we could pick up our handbags, excusing ourselves to go to the toilets en masse. Angie and Linda knew most of the local male talent, so I agreed to follow any lead they made. I had no intention of letting anyone pick me up anyway.

I wouldn't go so far as to say we did this telepathically. We watched one another's faces closely for the signals. One thing girls were good at was reading reactions. If one of us liked the look of a boy, she could choose to stay. So, if I fancied someone, but they didn't, they would leave me to it, and vice-versa. The hope was then the guy interested in you would stay and his mates would drop out. If it didn't happen, you could excuse yourself, pick up your handbag, and walk away to re-join your friends. The boys would instantly break up the circle retreating to the edges. Boys dancing with boys was a big no, no. All so different from the way men had approached girls back in the 1940s when I went on the prowl.

Linda's boyfriend, Steve, joined us with Tom Catford. Tom was every inch the tall, handsome, brown-eyed heartbreaker Angie had warned me about. Smart suited and shoed, I could understand why this tall young man had girls salivating over him. He acknowledged me with a surprised sign of recognition. Evidently, he had met Alice before, which confirmed Edie's tale. Tom barely had a dance. Carol dragged him away as the Isley Brothers *Take Some Time Out For Love* began playing. Angie whispered something to Linda. They grinned. Linda then whispered Carol and Tom were in the alcove behind me next to the DJ booth.

The alcove had seats for kissing couples. Glancing over my shoulder, I glimpsed Carol having her bust caressed by Tom as they kissed passionately. It should not have surprised me. The lip wrestling had started straight away, making for a rapid exchange of smirking glances between us.

A few whispered words to Linda and Angie dragged me off the girls' toilets yet again. "Let's give Linda and Steve some space. She's been going out with him for a while. He's not long been out of the hospital. Some bastards stabbed him when he went to Manchester shopping for blueys."

"Blueys?" I queried, puzzled.

"Purple hearts. Pills. Amphetamines. Drugs."

"Drugs? Really?" My surprise made Angie smile.

"I'll tell you all about it another time."

Bob and Earl's *Harlem Shuffle* started to play making us rush back to the dance floor. The record interrupted any further questions I might have asked. *Ride Your Pony* came on next on the DJ's turntable. Lee Dorsey, the singer had an unusual almost smoky, happy-sounding voice. I'd also heard it at Angie's and loved the effervescent way it made me want to dance.

Someone Angie clearly didn't like tried to approach us for a dance. She immediately picked up her handbag and I followed as we retreated briefly into the toilets yet again. I had to admit I was getting fed up with going in there with such regular monotony.

"I take it he's someone you don't like?" I queried breathlessly.

"Can't stand him. He's one of Ray's cousins. So," Angie began tactfully, changing the conversation as we heard the record finish, "seen anyone you like the look of tonight?"

"I haven't even bothered looking," I replied truthfully, checking the state of my lipstick and makeup in the compact mirror.

The new earrings gave me a chic look, but it came with a sudden penetrating awareness. Everything around me seemed to slow and freeze into momentary stillness. My actions had become so female I barely gave them a second thought any longer. Automatically using a compact to check my lipstick, admiring the new earrings, the girly chit-chat, it hit me hard. The moment forced me to shut my eyes tight. For the briefest instant, I wanted to wake from this reality and return to the man I had been. I couldn't. Phil Manley was well and truly dead, and I was someone else now. Only his memories lived on in me. I wondered if these memories were even mine anymore. They had started to fade into a kind of dreamy dimming fiction, like the browning pages of an old book. My new life had superceded my old one.

"Never mind." Angie continued, speaking earnestly in my ear, returning me from my frozen moment in time. "I'm worried about Carol. Tom Catford's a right, Casanova. The silly moo has had sex with him. And she wasn't even his first."

My open-mouthed look of surprise made her break out laughing.

"I wish you could see your eyes when I told you. They became the size of golf balls!"

"Stop exaggerating," I replied, miffed. "Isn't Carol scared of getting pregnant?"

"Her father is a barber. Carol told me she'd nicked a couple of packets of Durex from his shop. Just don't say I told you, which I know you won't." Angie paused, "I'll give him this much. Tom doesn't go bragging about his conquests. When he drops a girlfriend, the other lads are hanging around waiting to pounce to get off with her. They all know there's a chance of getting a leg over if they think she's not a virgin. Let's buy a coke before we start dancing. Stick close to me."

By the time the group came out on stage, tiredness had taken hold. Angie seemed unaffected, clapping enthusiastically as the group began to play. At one point, midway during the group's act, some cheeky article squeezed my behind. Packed like sardines in a tin, I couldn't work out who was responsible. The boy with his girlfriend behind me could not have done it. He had his arm around her shoulder, and she stood right behind me. It was my first experience of being groped, but it would not be my last. Would I have hit whoever had done it with my handbag? No. Would I have punched him in the face? Yes. Probably. Although, on reflection, a heavily filled handbag could inflict pain.

While I enjoyed dancing to records, I was less keen on seeing the group. *Root and Jenny Jackson were* local, from Mirfield near Huddersfield. The group wasn't bad, but my first experience of seeing them live came as a shock. The sound levels were deafening.

When the group finished and left the stage, Angie and I stopped for a while longer. This boy Mack had still not come to the club, and I could see her disappointment. We decided to go home, although Angie appeared reluctant to do so. The thought of the long walk back in the early hours didn't thrill me. To my surprise and delight, Angie insisted on paying for a taxi to get us to her house. She explained she rarely took the car to town on a night out, especially if it involved having a drink in the Vic. She didn't want to be caught drinking and driving.

After a cup of tea, we went upstairs and shared the bathroom, removing makeup and getting ready for bed. I expected to sleep on the bedroom floor, but Angie insisted on my sharing her bed.

"Don't worry. I'll sleep up against the wall. I always do. You can sleep on the other side and make a run for it if I try anything," Angie joked.

"Ah, but what if I try something? You won't be able to get away," I retaliated. "If I were a bloke, I might. You're a stunner, and I can see why the lads fancy you. A lot of them were giving you the eye tonight. Luckily for you, I'm not a bloke."

"If I were a bloke, I would most certainly do you." She teased straight back at me. "Count yourself lucky I'm not a lezzie."

With heavy eyelids, I struggled to keep chatting as we lay side by side. Yawn after yawn came from both of us. We talked about her friend Carol, expressing our concern for her. How could a teenage girl take such a risk? Angie sighed, then released another loud yawn. She had, so had other girls she knew. Most teenage girls fifteen and upward had these same strong urges. Only fear of pregnancy kept most from trying.

"It becomes an itch you want to scratch." Angie paused. "Your imagination runs wild. You dream of someone's lips on your boobs, the sensation of their hands on your nakedness. Those are the thoughts in your head. And don't tell me you haven't thought the same. We all do. We get turned on imagining them parting our legs and doing the deed. That's how nature has made us."

Angie was right. Nature had designed the female body for men to do that. We were receptacles for their spent passion. Gloomily, I concluded I only had three choices. Alice's body showed no sexual interest or enthusiasm when it came to girls. So much for lesbianism. While I tried to find the idea appealing, my new body didn't. There was always abstinence. I could try to suppress my sexual desires. Or I could be the woman I was supposed to be. Particularly when Lorna kept mentioning she would love to become a granny one day.

The uncertain nature of my sexuality was a problem, one I needed to resolve. Abstinence appeared my only sane option for the present.

Chapter 19

I'm Into Something Good - Earl Jean (Colpix PX 729B UK – 1964)

December 1966

If anyone had asked me, as a man, why women love jewellery, I might have resorted to some jokey reply. Possibly some comment like a girl's best friend being diamonds. Unconsciously, my new girly life led me to enjoy the idea of sparkly ornamentation. It started with earrings. Alice had a small selection. I wore them to avoid having my ears re-pierced in future. Earrings quickly became a favourite adornment, and wearing them was less of a chore and more of a pleasure. On Lorna's regular forays to local Church jumble sales, I found some incredible bargains. All for mere pennies and not only earrings. The art of mix and match became a talent I enjoyed putting to work. Jewellery, I already knew, enhanced and defined a woman's style.

Every morning, as I looked in the mirror, all I could see was an unbelievably pretty woman staring back at me. There was nothing I didn't like about myself. Vanity, thy name is Alice, I would sigh, delighting in my prettiness. My face had to look perfect. Whenever I set off from home, I wanted to be the prettiest I could be. I revelled in a strange confidence.

As a man, I had once believed women who preoccupied themselves with their appearance were superficial. In films, they were always the ones portrayed in this way. Briefly, I did wonder if I was turning into one of these vain and shallow females? Thinking back to a time before and after I started courting Ivy, most young women used it as a means of attracting a man. I was most definitely not in the market for a man. Though looking the most attractive I could, drove me with an exceptional passion. I had swiftly realised how potent a pretty young woman could be. The thrill of some man opening a door for me was a flattering novelty. Even more complimentary was hearing my first wolf whistle. Had the whistlers known I was a dead man inside this pretty shell, I wonder if they would still have whistled so enthusiastically?

In Search of Charm, a slim book I borrowed from the library, provided all the essential information I needed to enhance my looks. The author, Mary Young, ran her own modelling school in London. Her advice was the most sensible I could find. One might be born female, but you turned yourself into a woman.

In a few short weeks, I had acquired all the so-called vanities of women. My new hairstyle marked me out as a young Mod girl. Style preoccupied me daily. I gave more and more serious consideration to the slightest imperfections and flaws in my appearance. I also took to borrowing and studying fashion magazines in a way I could never have previously imagined. It didn't go unnoticed amongst my classmates or Edie. Comments about how I had changed since rising from the dead were frequent and laced with envy.

My past military training had come into play. Each day I arrived at school with my shirt and skirt ironed to perfection and guaranteed to make even the most fastidious girl feel embarrassed. From being incapable of doing my own makeup, I now applied it expertly. In fact, so adeptly, it even passed school muster without comment.

My problems with bitchiness had almost ceased but had not entirely disappeared. Janice Barrowclough usually stayed clear of face-to-face confrontations. Her ego and reputation had taken severe blows as other brave souls had fought back with comments of their own. Usually, these were prefaced with her new nickname, Pigsy. Any comments she made tended to stay with her hangers-on. Nowadays she rarely voiced them openly. Her infamous evil eye treatment made me grin and shake my head whenever I passed her. The occasional comment about my mixing with druggies originated from her rumour mill. I saw no point in denying I liked going out dancing at The Plebs. Somehow, she must have learned about my weekend activities from others. How, where, and from whom, I hadn't a clue, nor did I care.

Going out on future Friday and Saturday nights caused some unease at home. Truthfully, I cannot say Lorna argued with me as such. She did make it clear she wasn't happy and gave her reasons why. We discussed the entire issue in an adult manner. Doing otherwise would have served no purpose. The one thing I wanted to spare Lorna was setting a conflict in motion between us. Of course, I argued my side not as a seventeen-year-old but as an adult in teenage guise. In the end, Lorna had no choice. She conceded. I could go out, but I had to be home on the last bus. Being a middle-aged man in a young woman's body came with its limitations and headaches. Trying to act the age I was supposed to be, instead of had been, wasn't easy. As for going to an all-nighter again, I would have to ask Angie to let me stay over at her place. I couldn't see this as a problem.

I understood the anxiety Lorna had about my going out on the town. As a mother, I understood her concerns for my safety, which also made me concerned for Cathy. Inevitably, I had to make promises I would not let my schoolwork suffer, which I had no intention of doing anyway. I needed to pass the exams as these would be vital for any future career I wanted to choose. How else could I hope to care for my adopted family and for Cathy if I didn't have a good job? I intended to make this working lifetime a good one but doing what I wanted. Except, for now, I no clear idea what it would be.

Chapter 20

You've Taken My Woman – John Lee Hooker (Vee Jay Records 293 – 1958)

December 1966

Cathy and I met up on Friday night. We retreated to the Beefeater's basement coffee bar in the alleyway behind the bank. It was a better place to meet than the Vic Lounge or the Upper George. Not everyone could pass for eighteen. Underage Mod girls like Cathy had less chance of being embarrassingly thrown out of the pubs. The Beefeater was the only choice for our indoor meeting. On a cold December night, the coffee bar provided a warm retreat. It beat standing in George Square or walking around the town centre trying to keep warm. The cellar part of the coffee bar was a popular spot for Mods to hang out. After an all-nighter, it was always open first thing on a Sunday morning. The pill takers came here to come down from their drug-induced highs.

My daughter never could hide or disguise her true feelings from me. Tonight, she looked well and truly upset. Life at home had not been easy since my death. Relations between Cathy and the woman who had been my wife had steadily deteriorated. When Cathy arrived, there was no hiding the unhappiness in her face. Something was not right at home. We found some seats mid-way down the length of the coffee bar. I didn't need to prise anything from her. Tears forming, she could not contain herself, telling me her mother was sleeping with a former acquaintance of mine.

Eddie Garside had been a boozing companion. One who had come into my life when I was doing my regular rounds of the town pubs. Did I become irate on hearing Cathy's news? No. How could I? Our marriage vows had stipulated until death did us part. If my new life wasn't such a parting, then what was? Imagine a judge ruling on the status of our marriage? Annulled due to unprecedented circumstances.

Life without Ivy had become a life of freedom even with the restrictions imposed on me as a teenage girl. The only heaviness in my heart lay with my daughter. How could I remain in her life as someone who could no longer be her father but more like a friend?

100

Cathy needed to unburden herself, having accepted the predicament of our relationship. She wished the two of us could set up a home together. Deep down, for the foreseeable future, this was not a possibility. As we talked, I experienced an unexpected, weird, and worrying flashback to the evening of my death. Momentarily I was back in The Upper George, recalling the comforting beer haziness brought on by the fifth pint of bitter. Garside had gone to the bar to buy the next round. Something now aroused my suspicion on his return with the pints.

Harrison, my other boozing chum, had begun telling one of his awful jokes. Something about a man walking up to a bar with a large chunk of tarmac under his arm. Straight-faced, Harrison recounted how the barmaid asked the man what he wanted? The man replied, a pint of beer and one for the road. I recalled cackling aloud, proving when you're two sheets to the wind, anything can be funnier than it is.

That's when my mind sharpened. Did I imagine it? Did I see Garside slip something from his hand into my pint? Had I forgotten it? Or was I so light-headed at the time I never gave it another thought?

As the memory returned, the scene flooded back into memory. From the corner of my eye, had I seen him slip something in my drink? Or had my beer-hazed imagination affected my memory of the moment? Strange how the tiniest details of the event now reappeared more sharply focussed.

I remembered striking a light using a Captain Webb matchbox. Then stupidly I had almost lit the filter tip end of the cigarette. That was how drunk I had been. This was the last cigarette in the second packet of twenty today. Before setting off home I recalled thinking I had to buy more cigarettes for the morning. The nicotine craving calmed as I drew deeply on the cigarette. I tasted the smoke in my mouth as it surged into my lungs. The memory of it took me by surprise. It was so unbelievably real. For a brief instant, as though magically transported in time, the physical sensations from another lifetime flooded back. Seconds later, the most awful, agonising pain had struck me in my chest. I rose to my feet, gasping for air, before collapsing in a heap on the floor. The flashback had a cruel vividness.

Had Garside slipped something in my pint to cause my heart attack? Had he poisoned me?

"Have you seen the death certificate, Cathy?"

She nodded, puzzled by my question.

"What did it say caused my death?"

Cathy sighed. "It said coronary thrombosis."

"Can you sneak it out and let me see it?"

"Why?"

"I want to satisfy my curiosity, Cathy. After all, who gets to see their own death certificate?"

Death was not such a terrible experience. Dying was a different matter. To die from a coronary was devastatingly painful and not the way I would have chosen to go. Death had been a release from the pain.

Until this evening, I'd given no thought to my demise. In all honesty, I didn't want to think about it. Though I'd survived death by becoming Alice, I had expelled the memory of the ordeal from my thoughts. My talk with Cathy revived it. The possibility Garside may have poisoned me took hold. Had he been the cause of my death? Had Eddie Garside murdered me? If he had, why?

Ivy knew him from when he used to call for me on our way to the pubs. Garside had lived a few streets away. The man had separated from his wife. Or rather, he had left her and his two kids for another woman. If I recalled rightly, she had thrown him out too. Neither his wife nor the other woman wanted him back. It had never occurred to me he might fancy Ivy. She was no beauty, not rich, certainly not well off, and not exactly a merry widow.

My insurance policy would have covered repaying the mortgage. There was a tiny pension plus child benefit. Maybe a couple of hundred pounds in savings but nothing that would make Ivy a wealthy catch. No doubt Garside would see her as a roof over his head with sex and meals thrown in. Ivy would not be a gullible fool. She would not be taken in by him. I didn't give it long before she gave him the imperial order of the boot.

The more I reflected on the situation, the more annoyed and anxious I became. What if Garside had murdered me? What if that had been his plan? Kill and replace me in the home I had worked hard to buy and pay off each month? The more I thought about it, the more I gave the idea credence, the more it seemed to make crazy sense. I would never have described Garside as a friend. Garside had been a boozing companion, nothing more. As a man, I didn't have any close friends, only acquaintances and boozing pals. Once married, most men, me included, rarely kept up friendships the way women did.

One of the joys of being reborn as a woman was discovering the closeness and warmth of female friendships. Especially the ones in which I found myself involved. The need for constant reassurances was what brought women together. The downside could be the bitchiness you might also encounter. Unfortunately, where my possible murder was concerned there was no one with whom I could discuss it. Only Cathy knew who I had become. I didn't want to raise the idea of my being a potential murder victim with her. There were obvious reasons why I shouldn't. So, what were my options? How could I prove if Garside had murdered me *if that was what had happened?*

Had there been an autopsy on my body? If so, wouldn't the pathologist have detected the poison? My death certificate would have revealed it if they had done a postmortem. The pathology report would have led to a full-blown police investigation had they found anything. What if an autopsy had not been done? Surely, they would have performed an autopsy on my body? Not to have done so seemed improbable.

I had been in my late forties, in reasonable health, or so I liked to believe. Dying so suddenly and unexpectedly, without warning, would have warranted an autopsy, a postmortem, wouldn't it?

No wonder I became exasperated and irritable. The idea ate away at me when I returned home. My brooding mood did not pass unnoticed. Both Lorna and my sister wanted to know what was wrong with me. I made up various excuses about schoolwork. As it happened, my period was due and proved a further excuse. Maybe it did contribute to my irritability. The more I learned about hormonal changes, the less inclined I was to dismiss them. No wonder I became exasperated and irritable in the days that followed. The idea ate away at me. Paranoia gripped my imagination.

Cathy met me midweek at the coffee bar after school. She had managed to sneak my death certificate out of the house. There, in black and white, lay the proof I needed. Garside had not murdered me. A postmortem had revealed coronary thrombosis as the cause of my demise. I sat back, drained by the relief with Cathy, wondering what it had all been about.

Chapter 21

Jimmy Mack – Martha & The Vandellas (Tamla Motown TMG 599 – 1967)

New Year's Day. Sunday 1, 1967

Angie's eighteenth birthday party was where it all began. For me, it has always been the time and the place where the fates spun all our futures together. Here was where the embryonic New Breed came together for the first time. At this eighteenth birthday get-together, I met the three sisters who the world would one day refer to as the Halloran Trinity: Effy, Ellen, and Grace. This was where I finally got to meet Mack MacKinnon, and also Nate Silvers. In a few short weeks, all our lives would entwine in ways none of us could have envisaged.

Some friendships one can understand. They occur naturally, almost organically. Others appear unnatural and yet become natural forged by and for life. Angie's friendship with Effy Halloran proved to be such a friendship. Their incredible bond has endured because of the love they shared for Mack, but equally for their eerily deep friendship with one another. Most people could never understand how two young women could agree to share a man. The two often described themselves as sisters-in-love rather than sisters-in-law.

What can I say about Effy? I took to her the moment we met, likewise her sisters, Ellen, and Grace. Something immensely endearing about the three drew me to them without hesitation. They took to me too, and not because I was Angie's friend. We seemed like jigsaw pieces, destined to come together and become part of a close-knit group of friends.

Mack and I had an interesting first conversation. He tried to fathom me with that searching analytical mind of his as we spoke. I think I left him scratching his head trying to work me out, which was a good thing at the time. So let me be honest and admit I fell for Mack. Right there, right then. Yes, I fell for him, as many young women did then and have since.

The female in me was irresistibly drawn to him. I have often asked myself why? Still, I have no answer, even after endless introspection. Some years later, what happened between the two of us had an inevitability. Effy and Angie, I'm happy you don't hold it against me anymore. All our daughters take after him and are strong-willed young women like their father. We raised them that way.

What was it about Mack that had us all mesmerised? His smile? The Eyes? His Voice? The way he moved. Somehow these attributes combined to act like an enchantment, casting a spell on the opposite sex. Even now he still possesses the uncanny ability to listen intently to everything any woman says to him. Coupled with his innate intelligence his easy charismatic sexual charm still stirs female hormones. When I saw Mack for the first time, he triggered an electrifying response in me. One I could never have anticipated. He possesses an almost lethal charm where women are concerned. Had he been a predatory Casanova, he would have been a real heartbreaker. His respect for women largely prevented him from behaving like one. On his own admission, he has always confessed he's a sinner, not a saint.

The more I got to know him, the more I realised he was the kind of man most women wanted. At seventeen, he was more of a man than some who would never be if they lived to be eighty.

As for Nate? It took me a long time to know him. I can't say I trusted him in the beginning. When it came to business, Nate could wheel and deal like few others. In the cutthroat world of fashion, he carried one of the sharpest blades, having been schooled from childhood in its use. I knew Nate was gay as soon as I clapped my eyes on him. Not that I minded. Nature made him that way. You are what you are. Thankfully his Ying and Yang always seemed to stay in balance. As he became older and more settled with his long-term partner, Angelo, he softened. Neither Mack nor the others ever cared about his sexual predilection. They accepted Nate for Nate, and of course Sara, his sister, Mack's future protégé. It has never been a surprise that he and Mack became lifelong friends. Over time, I suppose we all did, despite some of the more wayward things Nate could get up to.

Nate was Nate. Nate is still Nate.

Cathy and I left the party not long after midnight, Ivy having let her stay over at my house. She had even told Cathy not to rush back in the morning. No doubt Ivy fancied spending some time alone with Garside over New Year's Eve.

Monday evening, while the family watched TV, Angie called. I was in the kitchen, revising Chaucer and learning quotes for the mocks. Something was not right, and Angie was not her usual self. It had to be boy trouble. Her downcast teary eyes said it all.

"Has his girlfriend found out about you two?" My guess paid off.

"I think Effy suspects something has happened between us."

"Which does not surprise me. Does Mack know she suspects you two?"

"Yes."

"Either you both confess, or you both say nothing. Those are your choices. Confession may be good for the soul, but in the cold light of the telling, it's a terrible idea. Denial is your best choice. Say nothing if your friendship with Effy is as strong as you believe. Otherwise, more harm than good will come from admitting the truth. That's my advice."

Thank heaven she saw the sense of the advice. The truth would come out soon enough. By then, their threesome relationship would have become a reality.

Angie had further rather intriguing news. She and the Halloran sisters would be modelling Effy's designs for a fashion shoot in Manchester. Nate Silvers had been impressed with her designs and Mack's photography. I couldn't stop laughing when she suggested modelling might be something I should consider. When I heard they would earn five guineas for a day's work, I took the idea far more seriously. When I heard they were giving serious consideration to using me as a model at the session, I couldn't believe it.

Chapter 22

January 1967

My birthday breakfast was a red-faced experience. Edie sat there munching her bowl of Sugar Puffs and guffawing between mouthfuls. Frank grinned as he recounted my middle-of-the-night antics. Lorna even had a smile on her face as she listened.

"Henry Cooper would be really impressed with them moves, our Alice. Bet you would have had him out for the count, flat on his back seeing stars."

I had no memory of any of this. Edie said I had climbed out of my bed and sleepwalked onto the landing. They had awoken to the sound of my dancing around in slow-motion shadow boxing.

"Who's Moorhouse?" Lorna asked, concerned. "I don't know anyone with that name?"

"Moorhouse?" I glanced at her, shrugging. "No idea."

When the RSM heard I'd had a few amateur boxing bouts as a teenager, I found myself in the company boxing team in 1939. When I was fourteen, I began attending a local boxing club. My father thought it would be good for me to toughen up. I suppose it did because I was no pushover as a boxer. Why the Sarge put Moorhouse in the ring, I have no idea. They should never have let him try out with me. He was no boxer and had no idea whatsoever about boxing. The lad was a likeable sort but a cocky little sod. My uppercut punch put him flat on his back ten seconds after the first-round bell rang. He went down like the proverbial sack of potatoes. They needed smelling salts to bring him around.

Poor Moorhouse died from his wounds during the Tunisian campaign. I had to watch him die slowly in terrible pain. In my infrequently reoccurring dreams, Moorhouse boxed like a pro. The fight never seemed to end. I could never lay a glove on him as he dodged my punches. I would wake up in a sweat, exhausted by the ferocious and frantic action of the dream.

Since becoming Alice, I had experienced none of the nightmares that had previously plagued me. The Moorhouse dream I experienced now had changed. It no longer resembled the one from my past. Last night it had transformed into a new nightmare, running in a never-ending angry loop.

Moorhouse looked different too. Grey, corpse-like, and stiff, his movements were almost mechanical. My uppercut punch kept repeating as I kept knocking him down flat on his back time after time. He refused to stay down, rising from the canvas again and again.

"I loved the way you thrust both fists in the air as if you had won." Frank grinned. "My little, sis! The boxing champ! Gosh, you were awesome and funny! You even looked like a proper boxer."

"Who knows?" I responded irked by his teasing, "I might have been a boxer in a previous life."

My words set him off laughing again. "The way you ducked and weaved in slow motion was pretty realistic! You were like a pro-boxer. That uppercut you kept delivering looked ferocious. I wouldn't want to be on the end of it. You would have floored Henry Cooper with a punch like that. Thank God they don't allow girls' to box. If they did, I could see you winning the Lonsdale sparrow weight championship belt."

Frank patted me on the head as he left the breakfast table, chuckling.

"Ha, ha, brother dear. Any time you want some boxing tips, I'll show you the right moves."

That only made him, and Edie laugh even more. Lorna did her best not to choke on her toast. "Time you were getting ready to go to Boots. Frank, you better get off too, or you'll be late. You don't want your weekend over-time pay docking. And ride carefully. The weather looks horrible and icy."

I had gone with Lorna and Edie to the January sales midweek in search of bargains. As a man, I would have done my best to avoid going. Now, I not only had to go, because it was expected, but I looked forward to doing so. Lorna had been putting money aside all year for the New Year sales. We came away with new bed sheets, towels, and three pairs of socks for Frank. Not exciting but necessary items. Edie got a couple of new white Aertex knickers, which did not thrill her. No wonder she looked displeased when I received my birthday present from Angie. A grown-up sexy lacy brassiere and matching briefs in a deep burgundy complete with a matching full slip.

During the morning, Angie dropped in to see me at Boots to wish me a happy birthday. Her unexpected visit allowed me to thank her for the gifts. She and the gang, including Mack and Effy, were heading over to an all-nighter in Manchester. An American group called The Spellbinders was appearing at a club called The Twisted Wheel. Uncle Den had loaned her the use of his Bedford van to get them there. I knew Angie would have liked me to go. With mock exams looming on Monday, there was no possibility. Exam revision had become the priority.

Sunday evening, while Lorna and Edie were watching *Sunday Night At The London Palladium*, Angie came around, looking exhausted and paler than usual. Even after sleeping the whole of Sunday afternoon, staying up all night had not agreed with her. Missing out on her beauty sleep had been worth it. She insisted on recounting the events of the night. And what a great night it had turned out.

First, they had managed to get an infamous local drug dealer arrested. Then, the atmosphere in the club had been nothing less than brilliant. The Spellbinders had been superb on stage. The night out had been topped by meeting Jimi Hendrix and getting his autograph. Someone told them he'd come from London to see the group. Angie grinned showing me his autograph scribbled on her Twisted Wheel membership card. He had even tried to chat her up.

What a tale she had spun, leaving me open-mouthed in surprise. Then came yet another surprise leaving me stunned.

Angie announced, giggling that she was going to work at a solicitor's firm in town. She was the new receptionist and filing clerk for Hardacre, Hardcastle, and Hewitt. The solicitor's firm where Pamela's father was one of the partners. Yet another one of life's coincidences.

We chatted for a short while, but I could see Angie was done in and ready for an early night. From her handbag, she took out a paperback book as she left to go home. With a huge beaming smile, she said, "Here, read this when you have a moment. This will come in useful sooner than you think."

I recognised the face on the cover and the title. *The Truth About Modelling*. Jean Shrimpton, the top fashion model, had purportedly written it.

My locks got tugged a few times on arriving at school. The girls in my groups soon filled my satchel with small gifts and cards. The rest of the day was not too bad either.

Our mocks on Thursday started with a vengeance.

The next couple of weeks proved demanding. Getting down to revising swallowed most of my time and energy. In some ways, sitting exams again proved a challenge. My previous life experiences gave me an advantage. What a typical eighteen-year-old might struggled to do was less so for a mature mind. Somehow, I managed to get through the mocks without too much stress and with decent grades. An A and two Bs looked good, but I could improve on these by summer.

My daily life continued much as normal. Dr. Piller remained a singular exasperation. Appointments to see her infuriated me, becoming the irritating bane of my life. By now, I had developed a working strategy when confronting her. I made use of an assortment of tactics to prevent her attempts to hypnotise me. This included creating a reservoir of memories of some of my school friends. The good doctor would not be able to check up on these.

After the mock exams, the Upper Sixth routine kept me thoroughly occupied. My friendship group had grown, and my popularity had increased even more. The girls in my groups seemed to enjoy my company, especially after I dealt Janice Barrowclough a final coup de grace. I'll give the girl her due. She did insist on trying to denigrate me.

What broke her finally was my response to her comment. "Since you know it all, you should know when to shut up."

My dismissive reply was simple, but for some reason effective, it hit home with unexpected force. "Shhh. No one cares what you have to say, Barrowclough."

Sharing a bedroom with a younger sister, it became inevitable she would discover me reading the book about modelling. Edie's opportunity to make fun of me gave her great pleasure. She took to prancing about the bedroom, continually teasing and provoking me by striking modelling poses. Still, I persevered and read the book cover to cover in a couple of hours. The memory of Angie mentioning the five-guinea fee kept reoccurring as I read it. A five-guinea earner in my present situation was worth the effort. As I finished reading the book, Angie's words came to mind. *It's going to come in useful sooner than you think.*

The idea of becoming a model became irresistible. I had the figure. I had the legs. I had the looks. Why shouldn't I make it as a photographic model?

Angie's dark horse lifestyle surprised me too. There were many aspects of her life she kept to herself. Her home life had been anything but happy these past couple of years. Her parents were in a constant state of open warfare, brought on by her mother's mental illness. Though she and Gill attempted to do their best to help, their parents proved too much in the end. Gill found it increasingly difficult to study for further qualifications and to cope with their parental warring outbursts. Her father's attitude didn't help. Matters reached a point when both Gill and Angie decided they could not cope any longer. Then Angie made a further revelation.

She had been going to Tech at night during the week for the past year to study for her O Levels. The thought of standing behind a shop counter had made her realise she could do better. Encouraged by Effy and Ellen Halloran, she was intent on sitting O Level exams in the summer. Exams she should have taken if she had not left school. Then came the final surprise.

Gill had rented a small terrace house in Siddal. The two sisters had moved in together. I was sorry to learn Angie had left home. To visit her now was a bit of a trek to their house in Jubilee Road. Angie did not come around as often to see me as she tackled moving, studying, revising, and a new job.

Angie confessed she had taken part in an amateur fashion shoot in a parish hall in Bradford. Mack had organised the photoshoot for Effy's A-Level portfolio. When I finally saw his first photographs, I knew he was a genuine bona fide talent. The snaps were a revelation. So too were the Halloran girls and Angie. They were born to become fashion and photographic models. What especially impressed me were Effy's designs. I could see what the fuss had been about. Her dress designs were stunning. Effy was a bright and highly talented seventeen-year-old with marvellous dressmaking skills to match her fashion designer skills.

After seeing the photographs of Angie and the Halloran sisters taken by Mack, I became hooked on the idea of modelling. My thoughts kept turning more and more to what modelling might offer me as a career. Critically studying photos of models presenting clothes, I understood what it would require to be successful. The secret possessed by the top models, though simple, would not be easy to master. They possessed an ability to make the clothes eye-catching, enabling the photographer to capture elusive mood moments. No matter what they wore, they created a relationship between the garments, the photographer, and themselves.

When Edie wasn't in our room, I took to practicing in front of the mirror, working on poses, exploring showing subtle emotions. I worked on my posture and the way I walked, stood, sat, and reclined. As I explored what modelling entailed, it appealed even more. The strangeness of my new life, a different gender, and a new body captivated me more than if I had been born with it. There was a narcissistic pleasure in looking at myself in the mirror as a woman who had once been a man. And because I had been a man, I was even more enamoured of my physical beauty as a woman.

Chapter 23

Memories Are Made Of This – The Drifters (Atlantic AT 4084 - 1966)

Easter Sunday – Easter Monday 1967

Not having a telephone was an inconvenience. With Angie no longer a short walk away, keeping in touch became harder. A great deal was happening that I knew nothing about until suddenly I did.

Sundays were dreary days. Everywhere was shut with nothing much to do. Easter Sunday was no exception. Frank always bought a couple of Sunday newspapers which we would end up reading at the breakfast table. Personally, I found *The News of the World* and *The People* little more than a waste of printer's ink and paper. Frank and Lorna enjoyed reading about all the scandals in what was more commonly referred to as *The News of The Screws*. This Sunday could not have been more different.

I think we four sat open-mouthed in silence for at least twenty seconds, struck dumb and staring at the photograph in the newspaper.

"Gawd!" Edie broke the stunned silence. "Look at this! It's Angie Thornton!"

The infamous Cromwellian photo had hit the news pages. There they were. The three of them had been caught by the camera in mid-flight. Effy's leg was thrown across Mack suggestively, her minidress hem riding so thigh high it almost revealed her underwear. Her sexy, come-hither smile was not helped by the lascivious look on his face. As for Angie, nuzzling his ear, her hand on his chest? The hungry man-eater look spoke more than words making it all look so erotically charged. I persuaded Frank to go and buy some of the other Sunday papers in case there was more. When he returned, it proved a good move as there was more to see and read.

Inside a couple of these newspapers the fashion pages had photos accompanied by short articles. These highlighted Saturday's fashion show held at the Moods Mosaic boutique.

The newspaper articles were full of praise. Effy Halloran was a rising star, a new young up-and-coming fashion designer. The dailies had more on Monday. There were photographs of Effy modelling her clothes together with Angie and two other well-known models. Among the photos snapped at the boutique opening, a half-dozen taken by Mack. His eye-catching photography had caught the boutique's fashion show atmosphere in a trendy, Mod way. It wouldn't end there as more items would appear mid-week.

Effy's designs as photographed by Mack featured in the fashion pages of two more dailies. Even before these midweek items had appeared, news of the Sunday photos had already broken among the local Mods.

Easter Monday, I found myself accosted as I arrived in George Square with Cathy. The Drifters were appearing at The Plebs to an anticipated packed house. At £1 a ticket, it wasn't a cheap night out. We had managed to get tickets, to see them. A large crowd of regulars had already descended on the Square, hanging around in groups. Scooters kept arriving until there was nowhere for late riders to squeeze into a parking space.

Stingray and Alan Holmes wanted the inside story of what had gone on in London, having spotted our arrival first. There was nothing I could tell them. I knew as little as they did. Linda and Carol approached me next, followed by others, curious to know what was going on. What could I tell them? I only knew what everyone else had seen in the newspapers.

An eerie spine-tingling sensation ran through me like a premonition. Something big, it seemed to warn, was about to happen involving me.

Yes, the photo caused a real stir among the Mod girls in the Square and later in the week among the girls in the Sixth Form. Most of the Sixth Formers remembered Angie, as did a few of the younger girls in school. In the following days, the gossiping circulated endlessly. I thought it wiser to keep quiet and not mention that Angie and I were good friends. It didn't last. Despite pleas not to reveal my friendship with Angie, Edie failed to keep her mouth shut.

The events surrounding the threesome that weekend in London commenced their meteoric rise to the top. The weird sensation I experienced was about to turn out true. We would find ourselves slip-streaming behind them and living lives in the fast lane in the coming months.

Setting all that aside, The Drifters turned out not to be the real Drifters. Paul Mountain, the club owner, was conned. Someone, I think it may have been Mack, said later they were a group called The Fantastics. Even so, they were good, and the packed club enjoyed the performance.

Angie visited me a couple of days after returning from London. She made me an offer I could not refuse. Would I be interested in modelling for Mack and Effy? Mack wanted to give me a test shoot at the weekend. If interested, she would drive me over to the studio in Bradford on Saturday morning. It meant I would have to miss going to my Saturday job. No matter how I tried to play it cool, the prospect excited me. Already, I could see the potential of what was happening. I rang work saying I was unwell and made the trip to Bradford. It turned out the most astute move I would ever make.

The test shoot went off superbly. Afterwards, we drove back to the MacKinnon's home. Effy and Grace had been living at Mack's while their parents were in Ireland. Mrs. MacKinnon made me feel welcome having heard good things about me from Effy and Grace. As we sat around chatting, I noticed Angie wearing a gold-coloured Lucite ring. Effy had one too, so it was no coincidence. The rings resembled wedding rings. The way Angie and Effy behaved around Mack, I knew something unusual had taken place. That something had brought the three of them even closer together. I was right. It surprised me Effy's sisters didn't catch on to what was going on right in front of them.

Mack developed the prints in the afternoon, so I saw the results before Angie drove me home. I could tell he was impressed by the results, but maybe not as much as me. Mack had made me look like a top professional model. Angie gave me a wink. Driving back to Halifax, she let me know I was joining them. There was no certainty we would have any modelling assignments, but it felt like we were all setting out on an exciting adventure together. And so we were, and sooner than we anticipated.

Two weeks later, we did our first catwalk show at Silvers Fashion in Manchester. The five guineas fee we each received on this first assignment was the most money I had earned since becoming Alice. It was the equivalent of working eleven Saturdays at Boots.

Keen to impress an American buyer, Nate, and his father had arranged for her to see Effy's range in Manchester. The buyer, Pearl Piper, was a single-minded bitch personified. I recognised this within minutes of meeting her. Behind the glamorous Texan exterior, Piper possessed an icy hardness. My parents had raised me to try to see the best in people. When it came to Pearl Piper, it proved impossible. The woman was unscrupulously ruthless and granite-hearted. No one could have foreseen the trouble which would arise from this fateful first meeting. Piper could not tolerate Mack standing his ground with her. Even less when Effy and Angie stood by him.

Our first overseas fashion shoot was a rushed, hectic affair. Luckily for me, Alice had possessed a valid passport from the time when she had gone on a school trip abroad. Her father had paid for it shortly before his sudden death. Luck was once more on my side.

114

Hester and I took to one another from the moment we first met at the airport on the way to Spain. On the flight to Valencia, we chatted with each other as though we were old friends. So began our long and close friendship. I did feel sorry for her as I realised what was going on.

Poor Hester. How uncomfortable she must have been knowing Effy and Angie saw her as a rival for Mack's affections. No sooner had they settled into their threesome arrangement than Hester appeared to intrude as a romantic interloper. Not that she ever admitted to me she had fallen for him. I just knew she had. Her eyes spoke everything I needed to know. All of us had fallen in love with him sooner or later.

Hester and I became even closer during the trip, sharing a room in the hotel. Our sense of adventure took us into old town Benidorm. On the night out, Hester, Mack, and I, forged a deep, unique bond of friendship. During our brief stay in Spain, Hester revealed to me her concern for Mack, Effy, and the girls. Deceit and intrigue were already being played out behind their backs. The truth leaked out soon enough. I found myself becoming privy to what was going on in the days and weeks following.

We all knew Hester was one of the established photographic models in London. She had worked in the States and travelled abroad extensively to Italy and France. What we did not know at the time was that Hester was Hester Hemingway. Her father, Eugene Hemingway, was an American multi-millionaire, industrialist, and tycoon. Hester told me all about her father, having first sworn me to secrecy. Somehow, she knew everything about the new deal Piper and her associates planned to foist on Silvers Fashions and Effy. AIC InStyle happened to be one of her father's many companies, and Hester had friends privy to what was going on.

Certain information had come Hester's way via her extensive personal network of confidants. She couldn't tell me what at the time, but she knew, or suspected Pearl Piper was up to her usual no-good ways. The woman was renowned for her dog-eat-dog dealings. As my friendship with Hester blossomed, I came to appreciate this extraordinary network of confidantes she had built up. It extended into all walks of life. What was uniquely astonishing was how someone of her age could have built up such an amazing network.

Piper and Hester had a history with one another. Hester had never forgiven her for what had happened between them. She intended to be around in case her worst fears concerning Piper turned out to be true. That's when I came to appreciate how much Hester craved true friendships. And, of course, her serious concerns proved correct. Even as we left for Spain, the wheeling and dealing had already commenced behind our backs.

These days Hester Clayton is seen as the hard-headed and formidable editor of *Mystique* magazine. She has been to *Mystique* what Beatrix Miller was to *Vogue*. Those of us who came to know her that year learned about another side of her. Hester had a tremendous depth of compassion for others. Especially those she believed were underdogs being exploited. Her sense of justice and fair play personifies the woman she is.

What happened in New York would not have happened without the Benidorm incident. Armed with the infamous Benidorm article, Piper and her cronies attempted to use it as a bargaining chip when making the deals with Effy and Silvers Fashions. I blame Charmaine's manager for publicising the Spanish non-scandal in the French press. Potential scandals have always flown into roost almost as soon they became known. These days scandals move even swifter no matter where they happen. What appeared in the French press proved the ideal excuse for the events that followed in the Big Apple. At the time, Charmaine was unaware of what her inadvertent revelations in the French press had caused. I'm pleased to say in its own way the so-called incident led to a close friendship. Charmaine is often referred to as the *La Bonne Amie* of The New Breed, and with good reason.

Chapter 24

The Snake – Maximillian (London HLX 9396 – 1961)

Undated.

Pearl Piper was one of those rare Sixties women who managed to claw her way to the top in a man's world. Icily ruthless, this former Texan beauty queen and model proved an arch schemer and manipulator. Nothing had been allowed to impede her rise to the top. Whispers of her relentlessly determined approach mentioned manipulative and coercive tactics. There were no limits to how low she could and would stoop. The truth of what happened in New York made me realise how horrendously awful some women could become in pursuit of power. She possessed a tigers' tenacity to equal the most ambitious of men. I could understand why Henderson hired her, but not why he never fired her over what happened.

Hester was already in New York when I called the number given to me in Spain. It had become apparent within a day or two that Piper intended to manipulate and control Effy, her sisters, and myself by separating us from Mack. At the same time, she was attempting to exploit the Silvers. Nate's father had ignored his son's warnings.

Alex Silvers health had rapidly become precarious. The man was not at his best when he arrived in New York. Nate knew the deal was rotten, but his father stubbornly refused to listen to him. Without Hester's intervention, Silvers Fashions and Effy would have lost out in the negotiations. What went on between Hester and Nate in New York I never did find out, and to this day, I still don't know. What I did learn was the two had been friends from childhood. Something appeared to bind the two closely together. Hester has never to this day explained what made them so close.

How Hester brought about her father's intervention was something else she never cared to share with me. Thank heavens she did persuade him to intervene. What leverage she used against her father to convince him to do the right thing, I can only guess. Henderson was in the business of business, and gaining an advantage over his competitors had made him successful. I did wonder if Hester had somehow pricked his conscience over Effy and Mack.

Piper's tactics were flawed from the start. Her failure came down to regarding Mack and the girls as teenage simpletons she could manipulate. By cutting Mack off and feeding lies about him to the rest of us, she hoped to cause a breakup between him and us. She clearly had little idea how close we all were.

Piper was a bitter and twisted woman who not only wanted to get her way but intended to have her spiteful revenge. Her actions in New York revealed her waging nothing more than a personal and petty vendetta. A vendetta waged entirely over words exchanged at their first meeting in Manchester.

What did Piper expect? Did she really think Mack would sit quietly twiddling his thumbs in a tiny apartment in New York? She made a serious error of judgment. Left alone, wondering what was going on, he was bound to work out something was wrong. How he found out so quickly has also remained a mystery, although I'm sure it involved Hester. Mack turned up unexpectedly at the St. Regis hotel, his anger understandable though misdirected. It led to an awful scene in the hotel lobby between him and Effy. When she ran to get away from him, Mack followed her and came across Piper in conversation with his father and Greg Williams.

I arrived in time to witness his vitriolic and very public assassination of Piper. No quarter was given, no words spared. He shredded Piper's reputation in public with a spontaneous surgical precision no politician could ever rival. Piper had not only underestimated him, but she had also underestimated Hester, Angie, and me. June Nightingale's biography of Mack pieced together what took place that day. Using carefully researched eyewitnesses accounts, it is as near a word for word retelling as we shall ever read.

This first trip to New York led to some other long-term consequences.

Piper's beau at the time was Seth Devane, a New York fashion photographer. Devane by name, vain and arrogant by nature. Piper had seen to it her lover would get the fashion shoot originally intended for Mack. The fee for the shoot was a lucrative deal. Devane was sorely in need of the money. His recent divorce had cost him a fortune in alimony. Piper was Devane's lover as well as the cause of his infidelity and subsequent divorce.

The so-called infamous Benidorm bedroom incident was the excuse Piper and her assistants at AIC used to strong-arm the deal. Since it involved Effy, Angie, and Mack as minors, Piper claimed it would make damaging publicity. This was utter nonsense. The Vietnam War and the Race Riots dominated the news and American public consciousness that summer. The misbehaviour of three young British people was of little public interest. Effy's convincing television interview put an end to any speculations. If anything, the subsequent advertising campaigns did more good than harm.

Piper's whole scheme had been provoked by sheer vindictive spite based on malicious hearsay. She had tried to use it as a lever in her dealings with Alex Silvers. Piper also planned something even nastier as part of her deep-seated grudge-bearing. She persuaded Devane to seduce Effy to break her relationship with Mack. Their attempts at a modern-day version of *Les Liaisons Dangereuses* backfired.

If Mack had known what had been going on during the shoots, Devane would have been dead before we left America. Fortunately, he never learned how Devane had tried to seduce Effy. Devine's face bore the marks of his unsuccessful attempt. Deep scratches on his cheeks and neck, together with Effy's bite marks testified to the ferocity of her resistance. In all honesty, the incident was as near a rape attempt as anything. Luckily for Effy, he must have thought better of the idea and stopped knowing she was a minor under US law. Piper tried to hush it up, doing her best to make the incident sound like a harmless misunderstanding. We all knew it had been nothing of the sort. That's when we finally acted, having had enough of Devane and Piper.

Grace and I tackled Piper after learning of the attempt from a distraught Effy. There was enough of the man left in me to pin Piper to a wall. Six feet tall, the Texan cowered as all five foot eight of me threatened to beat her to a pulp. The ferocity of the assault worked. There was genuine fear in her eyes. Afterwards, shaking with fear, she demanded Grace should act as a police witness to my assault on her. Grace laughed in her face, then kneed her in the stomach with astonishing ferocity. No witnesses, no proof of assault.

Like Piper, Devane never reckoned with us either. His conscience, or lack of it did not stop him from trying to seduce the rest of us. Before the incident with Effy, he had done his level best with each of us in turn. His surreptitious attempts to fondle our busts or casually slide his hand up our dresses during sessions happened all the time. None of us felt safe, not even Grace, who was fifteen at the time. The man was incapable of keeping his dirty-minded grubby hands to himself. The molesting had to be stop. His persistent and pathetic efforts to live out a fantasy as some kind of Warren Beatty led to my angered response. My fist left his nose bleeding and put an end to the groping. The snatched scissors in my hand, aimed at his genitals, further convinced him I was serious.

Piper received her real comeuppance at the society soiree held by Hester's relative, Amy Fitzgerald. I like to believe the rather subtle violence Mack employed that evening impressed Eugene Henderson. He must have regarded Mack differently after the St. Regis hotel incident. Beating up the band members of *Zorro's Mask* made him a legend. Although, later, Henderson was not too impressed with how Mack and Tom dealt with Konstantinos, the Greek shipping tycoon. The Konstantinos incident had serious repercussions, so too did the infamous Daubney Affair. No wonder Mack has long been a suspect over what happened to Devane during our visit to New York.

Without wanting to be repetitive, let me state once more, James 'Mack' MacKinnon was, and still is, the coolest young man I ever met. It would be too easy to dismiss him as just another fashion photographer of the Swinging Sixties. Mack's photographic talents have extended beyond fashion photo shoots. His Summer of Love in New York City, the Paris Student Riots of 1968, and the infamous Anti-Vietnam War demo photography in Grosvenor Square documented social and historical events. They also represent photojournalism at its finest. Many of these are to be found in his photographic books, also in periodic gallery exhibitions. His talents have also extended beyond photography.

James MacKinnon has gone on to make award-winning television commercials and music videos. In time he has scripted, produced, and directed feature movies. Whatever field of activity he chose to pursue, I have no doubts he would have been equally as successful. As far as I am concerned, Mack MacKinnon has always been a modern-day Renaissance man. Although, he has admitted to having a dark side. One prone to emerging when necessary.

Now I come to the point in my story where I have a confession to make and a mystery to clear up.

Seth Devane met his much-publicised demise at the hands of an angry husband in 1970. The newspapers described his killing as an execution, which is an accurate enough description. On learning of his wife's infidelity with Devane, a mentally disturbed Vietnam veteran named Kurtz took revenge. He emptied a fully loaded magazine clip into Devane from his service handgun. The bullets from the first magazine clip were fired strategically to maximise painful wounding. Kurtz then reloaded a second magazine clip to administer the final coup de grace. He shot Devane in the genitals once. Kurtz then planted the last round squarely between his eyes. I genuinely doubt few women mourned Devane's demise. The man was a

120

loathsome lecher who believed himself entitled to have sex with any woman who took his fancy. After his death, a host of revelations came to light from the various victims of his sexual assaults. Several were effectively rapes. The press also unearthed his connections with the New York Mafia to whom he had been in debt.

The mystery of who gave Devane the beating of his life in the summer of 1967 can finally be revealed. It was I.

Since the man is dead and his murderer known, I doubt the NYPD could make any charges stick. For one thing, there would be no physical evidence. I made sure of that at the time. In any case, many will still doubt my admission of guilt. A woman of my height and build could not possibly have inflicted such injury on a man of his size and build. While the assault took place, Mack, Angie, and the Halloran's were busy doing the famous Manhattan skyline photoshoot from Henderson's penthouse. None of them could have been involved. It was me. I was the one on the other side of Central Park committing the deed.

In my previous life, I had fought in battles against the Germans and Italians as a soldier. I had become an expert in unarmed combat, acting temporarily as the instructor to new regimental recruits. Devane stood no chance against me, even in my female body. For a youngish man of his age, he was physically unfit and, truth be told, cowardly.

There was no way he could have known who attacked him. Heavily disguised in all-black attire, I was anonymous. My face was face hidden under a black balaclava with a slit cut out for eyes.

He was an easy, unsuspecting target as he left his studio by the usual route, a fire escape at the back of the building.

A punch to his gut made Devane fold in half. A second punch to the face broke his nose. Several vicious kicks to his genitals followed as he fell to his knees screeching in agony. The third fist to his jaw shut him up and left him semi-conscious on the ground. That was when I decided to stamp on his hand. I admit, it was a particularly vicious thing to do and out of character. My intention was to teach Devane a lesson and to stop him from sexually molesting other young women.

The assault took no longer than ninety seconds or so. Devane had no time to identify me. Although later, I wish he could have known I had been the assailant. I didn't realise the extent of the damage I inflicted on him until I read about it on the plane flying home. In addition to his broken nose, I had fractured his cheekbone and caused severe ligament damage to his right knee. This last injury happened when I stomped on his leg several times to prevent him from getting up. I also left him with severe contusions to his lower abdominal region. I did not think I had so much strength in my female body to do that amount of damage. It pleased me to be proved wrong and to know it would be some time before he used a hand-held camera again.

Do I regret my action? Have I regretted it? In all honesty? No. My conscious has remained strangely clear. Devane had it coming. It was the one occasion in my life when a streak of deliberate cruelty possessed me. I was driven with an uncontrollable passion and fury to inflict pain. Had Devane known why the assault had taken place, his attitude to women might have changed. Personally, I doubt it. It probably never occurred to him to ask why it happened. Maybe he reasoned this was a case of his being in the wrong place at the wrong time. The NYPD did not think so. They took the trouble to send a police lieutenant to London to question both Mack and his father. Father and son had alibis with Eugene Henderson as one of the many witnesses that night. No one ever suspected little old me. Why would they?

My vigilante days ended with Devane. Though, I admit, I came close to doing a repeat with Simon Silvers. First at Picasso's and later at the *Mystique* launch night in Bloomsbury.

When Bob Dylan sang about the times *a-changing*, he was right. The times were changing for women. We were experiencing new kinds of freedom. These, in turn, would lead to the start of the Women's Lib movement, my generation's effort not to remain the second-class gender.

No doubt you'll be thinking how could you, as a man in a female body, feel this way? The stark and simple answer? I had no other option except to be who I had become. I was not a man in drag. Nor a man who had undergone a sex-change operation. I had once been someone who had occupied a male body and who now lived out a new life in an acquired female one. My mind no longer experienced me as a man but wholly as a woman. When I looked in a mirror, I saw only me. I was Alice.

We were all glad to return to London from New York. Hester insisted I move in with her. A kind offer I could not refuse. We were ideal companions for one another.

The New Breed was going to be in demand. Hester's assessment of our futures proved one hundred percent accurate.

Chapter 25

I Live The Life I Love – Willie Parker (President PT 171 – 1967)

August – September 1967

Even before we had a chance to recover from jet lag, I remember Jane MacKinnon ringing in new assignments almost as soon as we had landed. Then more came in daily in the following weeks. There was no way I could have continued to live in Halifax and work in London with such schedules. Ellen had tried and found it impractical. The move proved far from easy. Not only because Lorna did not like the idea of my working as a model, but also because it meant my having to move to London. She still hoped I would take up my place at York University. The money I earned made going to university unlikely. In a few short months, my earnings were heading into the stratosphere.

When my A-Level results came through, I was pleased by the two A's and a B. My French O Level repeat must have staggered the French teacher. Alice had narrowly failed it three times. On this, the fourth attempt, I achieved a Grade 1. The highest possible grade achievable.

Pamela and Marjorie were the last girls from my group I remember seeing as I left Crossley & Porter. Shocked into disbelief, they had gasped when I told them I was already working as a full-time fashion model in London. My university place would have to wait. I had always wanted to go to university, and something I finally got to do, although not until later in my forties. The opportunity to earn a lot of money was here and now, within my grasp. It would have been a folly to give it up. Modelling would make me a wealthy woman.

I had come across a quote attributed to Marilyn Monroe, which neatly summed up my state of mind at the time. *"A wise girl knows her limits. A smart girl knows she has none."* Not only did it seem to apply to me, but equally as much to all the young women in The New Breed.

There was no way I could have ignored the lure of fame and fortune. To become a successful fashion model was something else. Beyond the money, there was far more to my decision. The girls in New Breed were not only my close friends. They were becoming my second family. Besides, I had acquired an additional new mission in life. I now believed it my duty to act as a kind of guardian angel to them. The need to be near to them became an imperative after what had happened in America. My newly acquired status as an international model came with a whole new baggage load of demands.

It's too easy to believe modelling is simply about sticking on false eyelashes, applying some war paint, and then performing a few flounces in front of the photographer. There is so much more to being a top model. As Sharon Tate was reputed to have said: *A pretty face isn't all that important. It will open doors, but that's it. You have to have talent to back up what you have going in front.* She was right. As a model, you must have a personality with an innate understanding of what it is you are doing. For a young woman, it can be a worthwhile profession, even if a short-lived one.

Unfortunately, being a model in the Sixties carried stigma by association. The comments made about modelling nearly always mentioned how much money models were paid (too much). Or they were looked on as working at something regarded as shameful, even disgusting. Modelling had an undeserved and unwarranted reputation, only marginally better than prostitution or pornography. Perhaps women like Christine Keeler and Mandy Rice-Davies encouraged unfair treatment by the press. Lurid revelations about their private lives probably did no favours. It gave a rather unfair view of all the rest of the profession. Although, I must admit, not entirely without justifiable cause in a few instances.

Ellen Halloran and I did receive offers to do pornographic sessions. We laughed at the men and told them what they could do with their suggestions. The two of us became skilled at dealing with and heading off similar approaches, which we passed on to younger models. I will admit Playboy Magazine did approach me, but I turned down their offer to appear as a centrefold.

Avoiding men with sex on their brains was a never-ending battle of wits.

Our good fortune as models came about because we were young and part of the same generation of older teens who saw themselves in us. Only a few who became models ever achieved the levels of success like we did as the New Breed. We were somewhat like pop stars in a famous group. Pop stars depended on hit records for their success and earning power. The more hits they had, the more money they made. The more assignments we had as models, the more we earned. If you were in demand as a model, you were in the money. You also achieved fame and sometimes notoriety.

When it came to working, there were some days when I found myself doing as many as three sessions. Often these could be with three different photographers in different London studios. A couple of times in New York, I did four sessions. Some of these could take three hours, requiring different makeup and hairstylists at each.

Much of our success was due to the arrival of *Mystique* on the magazine racks. We had the good fortune as new faces to appear in all the usual top fashion magazines of the day like *Vogue, Harper's Bazaar, Queen, Elle,* and many others in the USA and Europe.

There were a few quiet times in the working year. December and January could be slow, as could some of the summer months, especially August. Somehow in the first few years, even these months did not turn out to be at all slow.

My memories of those late Sixties years are of travelling extensively abroad on magazine assignments. Those were the best ones, but also the most tiring. The clients paid for everything, from the airline tickets to the hotels and meals. Pay came on top, almost like an added bonus. Some of the locations were fantastic: Greece, Italy, the South of France, the Bahamas, and naturally New York. My most memorable and enjoyable assignments were the ones in Japan, Australia, Hawaii, and California.

When we first became models, the girls and I were delighted to earn five guineas for the day. Within months we found ourselves being paid staggering sums, especially in the USA. Much of it had to do with Angie Thornton's outrageous demands for higher rates of pay early on. I still blush with embarrassment at her brazen deal-making. Back then, a good model could expect to earn around fifteen hundred pounds a year which was very good money. Some, like the very top models, could earn as much as ten thousand. In my first year, I took home six after tax deductions. I never earned less. My average earnings after 1968 were much higher. Only my best-selling novels made considerably more money.

The public doesn't appreciate that as models we are self-employed. This important piece of information escapes most people's notice and hardly ever receives a mention. The fact is we all pay an agency fee for each assignment we receive. The agency can skim as much as fifteen percent off the top of our assignment fee. Our gross earnings are the figures that usually make the headlines. No news article ever mentions how much we are taxed. We also need an accountant to deal with the Inland Revenue. Accountant's fees are another extra outgoing.

My life as a new model back in those years seemed frenetic. All I recall is a blur of rushing from one studio to another by taxi. If not to a studio, then to never-ending hairdressing appointments or a design salon for special fittings. Whatever I did, I always had to remember to get receipts wherever I went for my accountant, Jane MacKinnon. Then there was the non-stop bag checking to ensure I had everything I might need on an assignment.

Every model back then carried a huge bag to a job. These had to contain everything a model might need to prepare for a session in addition to hairbrushes, a hand mirror, you had to have selections of hair slides, ribbons, different styles of wigs in assorted colours. No bag was complete without a selection of these wigs and hairpieces. Our makeup bags contained: false eyelashes, eye shadows in different colours, eye pencils, mascaras, lipsticks, blotters, brushes, and anything else we might need in every conceivable shade to suit a given skin tone.

Then there was the underwear: full slips, half-slips, flesh-coloured bras and briefs, white bras, strapless bras. If you were doing a knitwear advert for a jersey or a knitwear dress, your white bra might show under it. So, the flesh coloured one was not only a necessary standby but vital. You also had to have body stockings, a selection of tights in various shades such as sheer, sparkling, and textured. The money I spent on new tights and stockings became ludicrous, but at least they were considered tax-deductible.

The best tip I received came from Mack. Whatever you wore underneath the dresses, blouses, skirts, trousers, and so on, you needed to ensure no underwear lines showed through. Common sense, but it was all part of the learning game, and we learned rapidly.

Oh! And the shoes! We needed at least three pairs of casuals ranging from light to dark. However, on the top assignments, they generally supplied expensive makes in the latest styles. Too often, they did not get the sizes right. One day I might get bunions because I had to squeeze into the poorly fitting shoes that they provided.

The downside of working as a photographic model is that you had to wear what they told you to wear. Some of the Avant-garde fashions I modelled were laughable. These jokey creations were wholly impractical for anything but exotic fashion magazine splurges. Some of the incredible hairstyles they created could only be achieved with hairpieces and wigs. These supposedly futuristic coiffures looked utterly ludicrous. They were totally impractical hairstyles fit only for a fashion shoot. I hated these enormous bouffant styles, and they took ages to create. Learning how to keep them on your head so they looked natural was another matter. Let me state for the record these creations were not of our choosing but the far-out hare-brained imaginings of the stylists and photographers. Pity the poor girl who wondered how she could achieve such a thick, luxuriant mane like the models.

Nor did anyone ever warn us about how to slip into a tight-fitting dress to avoid messing with the hair stylist's latest crowning confection. We had to perform like contortionists to put on these outfits after our hair and makeup had been done.

The New Breed bad hairstyle awards started as a joke. Stella Lane had appeared in an advert with the most absurdly massive bouffant hairstyle. We began the competition for the silliest hairstyle of the year as a bit of fun. I took the 1968 award, although I reckon it should have gone to Ellen Halloran. Still, the girls all chipped in for a half-dozen bottles of Bollinger as the prize, which got all of us merry later that evening at Hester's. The world of fashion was not only hard work, lucrative but surprisingly enjoyable most of the time.

The creative skills demanded in fashion design were not only practical but also artistic. To this day, I remain amazed at how Effy mastered all the skills of a fashion designer. She possesses a staggering wealth of talent, combining traditional skills and innovative artistic creativity.

Effy taught me to understand fashion at a deeper and more meaningful level. She has always read prodigiously. Through her love of literature, she introduced me to Virginia Woolf's novel, *Orlando*. It was by accident and not design. Effy had taken to keeping notebooks with quotes, a habit she acquired from Mack. One day she read me these two quotes.

"Vain trifles as they seem, clothes have, they say, more important offices than to merely keep us warm. They change our view of the world and the world's view of us."

In my opinion, the quote is a truism. The clothes we wear announce to the world who we are. Your personal style reflects you. It can also reveal your personality and sometimes even your attitude to others.

The second quote had my full attention.

"For here again, we come to a dilemma. Different though the sexes are, they intermix. In every human being a vacillation from one sex to the other takes place, and often it is only the clothes that keep the male or female likeness, while underneath the sex is the very opposite of what it is above."

Now I do admit Effy was generalising about the sexes and fashion. She wanted to make a point about trouser suits for women. She happened to be

127

adjusting a trouser suit, one of her designs at the time, to fit me for a shoot. What sparked my interest in *Orlando* was knowing it was a novel about a man who transformed into a woman. I persuaded Effy to loan me her copy. There was a great deal more for me to ponder after reading it.

Part of the glamour of being a successful model was the inevitability of finding yourself wittingly or unwittingly drafted into the life of the celebrity circus. Adapting to the Sixties celebrity circus was a necessary evil, as we all discovered. Thank heavens we had Hester as our Dante like guide and mentor to the celebrity inferno and its denizens.

Did men lust after me? Yes. I know they did. What would have been their reactions had they known the truth about me? I smile every time I think about the possible reactions.

Chapter 26

You Turn Me On (Turn On Song) – Ian Whitcomb (Capitol CL15395 – 1965)

Undated

My first tentative foray into sex took place one Saturday night at The Plebs. Curiosity had gotten the best of me. I now felt fully female and ready to test my sexuality. He said his name was Mike. Dark-eyed Mike had been watching me dancing for some time with Carol and Pamela. Like most young men in their late teens, he had a decidedly nervous look wondering what his chances of success might be.

Carol had quite fancied the young man herself having been ditched by Tom in favour of Ellen. Mike showed no interest in her. Instead, he kept up a stream of inconsequential chatter avoiding silly chat up lines. Pamela eventually dragged Carol off to the toilets leaving me with the young lothario. When a slow record started playing, I found myself embraced dancing cheek to cheek. It flashed through my mind I needed to go through with what was about to happen next. When the record finished playing, we went off to the side next to the alcove by the DJ booth. There was nowhere to sit. Every seat had been taken by kissing couples. The next thing I knew, I had my back to the wall and his lips met mine.

The experience turned out nothing at all, as I expected. I was surprised at my reaction to our kissing. The sensation was wet, warm, and slippery, the way it had been between Ivy and me when we were courting. My body seemed to be giving me peculiar flutters, signalling I should enjoy what was happening. I had expected to find the experience awkward, half imagining teeth clashing on the first contact. Fortunately, it did not spoil the pleasure of my first kiss as a young woman. Yet this young man proved quite sweet and behaved himself. He made no attempts to touch my bust or behind, nor to French kiss me. I could not avoid his swelling bulge trying to break through his trousers as he pressed himself against me. In a way, I was relieved because I had wondered how I would react to the experience. Whatever remained of my masculine memories harboured nervous reservations, but my feminine side was now in charge and enjoying the sensations.

Years later, I would learn that the male and female brains functioned differently. When I took over Alice's body, I inherited her brain as a residence for my mind. What I didn't understand at the time was how a teenage girl's brain chemistry worked differently from a teenage boy's. My female side had subtly and unobtrusively altered my male thinking and biological responses.

A year later, I lost my female virginity with one of Hester's male acquaintances. I thought it was about time I did. By then, I'd kissed and cuddled a few, but I now wanted the complete sexual experience.

He was older in years than my female self, divorced, in his late twenties, and needing a physical outlet for his sexual desires. It wasn't about love or even about me having an affair. For him, it was all about the sexual release with more than a touch of lust. For me, it was practicality. He had the experience to make losing my virginity a satisfying experience. One thing was sure. He knew his way around a woman's body and expertly performed what was required.

At the time, and I must be honest, the idea of being penetrated by a penis created a few issues for me. My acceptance of who I had become was pretty much complete. Nevertheless, memories of having sex with Ivy as a man remained. Especially our first time together after we were married. I had no intention of letting those memories stop me from having a new sex life as a woman.

There were no misgivings about losing my female virginity, although looking back I wish it had been with Mack. Whatever apprehensions I had beforehand, I mentally set aside. Anyway, once done, having sex as a woman never caused me any more problems. Yes, it proved painful the first few times but also uniquely pleasurable. After losing my female virginity, it surprised me how my past life as Phil Manley became even less tangible. Had it not, and had I allowed my old life to dominate my new, it could have led to eventual madness. Acceptance of my fate was always the key to being Alice.

My love life as a woman flourished after that and proved sufficiently varied and enjoyable. Not that I made a habit of sleeping around. My sex life was highly selective and always serial. I knew all about the dangers of venereal diseases from my soldiering days. In the late Sixties the clap was rife in celebrity circles. Sex was one thing. Settling with someone was something else. Perhaps, I was too particular. Or maybe I yearned too much after Mack. I have never found that someone else. There was no substitute for Mack. Angie and Effy did, in the end, allow him to share some life with our daughter and me in much the same way as they had with Joy.

A year or so later, I couldn't resist picking up a copy of Gore Vidal's recent novel, *Myra Breckinridge*. The novel had caused controversy. As a biting satire, it had something to say. I understood why on reading it. Some lines created an immediate impact. One quote has left my thoughts unresolved even now.

"Of course, magic was involved at the beginning of my quest. But I have since crossed the shadow line, made magic real, created myself. But to what end? For what true purpose have I smashed the male principle only to become entrapped by the female?"

I still wonder if that was a part of my intended purpose. Was I entrapped as a female for such a reason? Thinking back, perhaps I had been trapped as a male. Perhaps finding myself as a female, I had in some way become liberated. Or was my life as a female one of being trapped too?

As a man, I remember experiencing loneliness. I didn't realise its pervasive extent in my life. Men, as I have said, though they have friendships, rarely enjoy deep, rich, and personal friendships like women do. It was certainly not the done male thing of my generation to have such deep male friendships. At least not in my past life's experience. No doubt some men will disagree strongly with my last comment.

Whatever gender we are born with, we are trapped within its bodily confine. In our minds, we can feel genderless. The fact is you can never escape the biological reality reflected in the mirror. You are what you see. Daily existence always brings you back to your biology. As much as we would wish otherwise, our biology does define who we are.

Hester taught me so much about what it meant to be a modern woman as well as a friend. She introduced me to more than the world of modelling. Through her, I came to know all there was to know about this wealthy layer of people who leached off the rest of society. These were the lotus-eaters who contributed nothing to benefit the vast majority toiling away for a livelihood. The indolent and parasitic lazy rich was a stratum of persons Hester despised. She opened my eyes and showed me these people in their natural habitats. Like her, I came to detest them too, wanting to see them condemned to the fourth circle of hell. Thanks to Hester I understood wealth came with a price and responsibility.

Chapter 27

Wasn't Born To Follow – The Byrds
(From 'The Notorious Byrd Brothers' LP CBS 63169– 1968)

Undated.

When the younger generation ask if I was a hippie, I laugh disparagingly. I think this notion may have stemmed from some of the fashions I modelled in 1968. When I look back on the images now, I understand the reasons for the misunderstanding. The outfits had either an ethnic look or quasi-fantasy-coloured kaleidoscopic prints supposedly representing some sort of psychedelic experience. Add the headbands and bandanas, and we created the Hippie illusion. Designers were keen to cash in on the Hippie flower-power bandwagon. Where I was concerned, nothing could be further from the truth.

We were being paid a great deal of money to shoot these fashions and on location. Quite a few of the best photos from these shoots took place in California. The ones I loved most we took on the outskirts of Carmel near Monterey. In fairness, Mack made the Hippie photoshoots appear amazingly authentic. They had a look of photojournalism, and these found their way into quite a few magazines. He also took some outstanding beach shots in Carmel. I have never looked as good in a bikini since.

Our friendship deepened on the Californian road trip. Those tentative first steps would eventually lead to a more intimate relationship.

In all fairness, the Hippie dream was a short-lived fantasy. It never caught on in Britain. The climate, for one thing, hardly matched California's sunny disposition.

Genuine Hippies in Britain were few. They probably found living the lifestyle almost impossible. Only the Aristo-Hippies in the media conjured up the lifestyle as a possibility. These back-to-land aristos had hefty family bank balances to cushion their Hippie visions. The backing of a press looking for sensationalism skewed perceptions.

As the decade ended, this counterculture proved a mirage practiced by very few. Those without financial resources who tried living such a lifestyle soon discovered you still needed money. No, only the rich pursued the Hippie dream on the highways and byways of England. A few took the

Hippie trail to Kathmandu in the Himalayas. The rest played at living the dream. They could chant peace, love, and anti-materialism while the press exploited their outpourings, often with sardonic intent. It became a myth perpetrated by reporters and journalists. It was an even bigger myth that these Hippie dreamers did something for nothing. Without money, the Hippie dream of self-sufficiency was at best a fiction, and at worst, a lie. The idea of becoming a Hippie appalled me then as it still does.

Most of the New Breed came from hard-headed Northern backgrounds. We were raised to believe you had to work hard to get what you wanted in life. An attitude typical of most young Mods, in fact. Only Hester came from a privileged and wealthy background. Early on, even she had decided to try and make her own way in the world. Her difficulty lay with her multi-millionaire father interfering too much in her life. He attempted to manipulate her from afar. There had been friction between them as a consequence. Only in the preceding year, before we first met did Hester and her father begin to make up and come to an understanding with each other.

Like Hester, we young women in The New Breed had determined to make it on our own. We were all single working young women, not the wives or girlfriends of pop stars with unlimited access to money. Our ethic was to work hard and to work for every penny we earned.

Nothing much changed for most people in Britain. They remained unaffected by Hippies as their lives focussed on more down-to-earth daily life. Only the illusion of change in society somehow came to be associated with the Flower Power generation, thanks to the media. Many in Britain regarded the whole counterculture as a bit of a joke.

As for women and free love? It came with the usual strings and not just in these Hippie communes. Women were still the ones who had to put up with unchanging male attitudes. Men continued to expect women to carry on with all the usual domestic duties. Chores such as cooking, washing, cleaning, providing sex on demand still remained most women's lot. So did taking care of any children resulting from the sex. It saddened me as a woman to see their roles remaining relatively unchanged.

The Manson Murders and the Hells Angels stabbings at the Altamont Pop Festival in Monterey have become the go to reasons why the flower power movement and the Sixties died. The fact is it had already died, even before the Sharon Tate killings. The Manson trial finally ended the dream, or so we are often told. I don't believe that to be the historical truth. The dream was already dead. Here and there, a few hippie communes persisted. For most, the flower power dream proved unsustainable. More so in Britain, where only a few die-hards struggled on and where the climate ruthlessly culled others. For most British people, the Hippie movement was disregarded and dismissed.

Chapter 28

Will You Still Love Me Tomorrow – The Shirelles (Top Rank 540 – 1961)

Undated.

Women are hardwired from birth with a kind of internal radar to read emotions in others. I like to refer to mine as *femdar*. My 'femdar' was something I experienced almost immediately on becoming Alice.

How can I best describe it for the benefit of men? In the beginning, detecting emotional reactions in others took me by surprise. My ability to see subtle emotional changes in others had suddenly become acute when I became female. At the time, I didn't quite understand what was happening to me. The more time I spent in the company of women, the more obvious it became that female empathy was a kind of extra sense. It made me realise how in comparison, many men lacked all but the most superficial empathetic ability. Most men seemed unable to detect, let alone read, subtle changes in emotions and moods. For many single and young men, empathy, if they possessed some, was largely superficial and under-developed. Married men, I noted, tended to improve the longer they lived with their partners.

During our last few days in New York, Hester and I became seriously concerned with Effy's state of mind. Our *femdar* had detected something amiss. On returning to London, Mack, Angie, and Effy were busily intent on finding flats. Angie and Effy wanted two separate homes in the same building. Each believed in having a nest of her own with Mack so that he could shuttle between the two. That was the plan and typical of the strange nature of their personal lives. Like myself, they needed to base in London. Hester was keen to have them living close by, as was I. At the time, I didn't understand why she was so keen for them to be near. It had everything to do with the business, but it was all about friendship. Hester, with her connections, had arranged for them to view some flats. I think she had a hand in making sure they took the ones in Radnor Walk.

The plan had been for the threesome to stay over in Grosvenor Street in the small flat belonging to the Silvers. After a single night, Effy persuaded Hester to let her stay with us in Sloane Gardens. Effy's pretext was that Mack and Angie needed some time together. That was not entirely true. Effy was in a state of anguished turmoil.

The brief falling out between her, Mack, and Angie had affected Effy more seriously than we all suspected. We could tell something was not right with Effy that morning as we readied for work. Hester had a meeting with her mother at the new *Mystique* offices in Soho. I had an early shoot in Swiss Cottage, which I hoped would be over quickly. Effy was supposed to be down at the Moods Mosaic boutique for a meeting with Nate and Simon. As soon as my shoot was over, I planned to have lunch with her. Hester would try to join us as soon as she could.

With my session over, I took a taxi to the boutique. On arriving, I learned Effy had set off to meet Simon Silvers at Picasso's coffee bar. She had apparently forgotten we were supposed to meet for lunch. Tina Wood, the manager, told me Simon Silvers had not arrived for the meeting at the boutique. At his suggestion, Effy had agreed to a late meeting with him at Picasso's. My arrival there proved timely.

I'd never met Joe Silvers or his younger brother, Simon. Hester couldn't stand Joe and didn't care much for Simon either. Joe was on trial for attempted murder at the time. As far as Hester was concerned, Simon came out of the same mould as his brother. The young one had already acquired an unpleasant nastiness disguised by a superficial sheen of gentlemanly behaviour. Like his older brother, Simon belonged to a generation of men who believed in their entitlement to have sex with any woman who took their fancy. The Alfie syndrome was rife in those days. All women were regarded as fair game. Simon Silvers attitude to women was by no means unusual.

Effy had fallen in love with Mack when they were young. Their love affair was born in trying circumstances, and it was a truly romantic love affair. How she and Angie came to share Mack was something emotionally deeper. This threesome love affair could only have happened to them. None of us ever believed it would last. Yet, strangely enough, it has and remains an extraordinary relationship enduring as strongly as when it first began. For most people, it's always about finding that one special person. For them, it has always been about being the three, or at times, the four, and even five.

Although she always denied it, I believe Effy was briefly attracted to Simon Silvers. I imagine this attraction was most likely frivolous and superficial. Grace always thought her sister had taken a fancy to him. I believe the idea of having sex with someone else was a fantasy for Effy. She confessed as much when she told me she couldn't help wondering what it would be like to sleep with another man. This was not the first time I'd heard a woman say something like this, nor has it been the last. Men seem oblivious to the idea that women have fantasies, not just them. They do, and they are as vivid and varied as that of any man. Women are equally as tempted to see if the reality is anything like the fantasy.

After New York, Effy wrongly believed her relationship with Mack and Angie was falling apart and ending. The temptation to have a fling must have filled her thoughts. Perhaps it was as though doing so might provide her with an escape route if everything did fall apart. I suspect she may have reasoned, if someone like Hester could sleep around, why couldn't she? The events in America had pushed her young, inexperienced mind into brooding despair. The American trip had been nothing less than a nightmare for her. If not for Hester, who was the true heroine of the day, Effy and Silvers Fashions would have lost out, so too would Mack.

My arrival at Picasso's proved timely. Silvers was in full Casanova mode, busy weaving his spell of seduction, trying to get her back to his place. He never noticed my arrival or was aware I was overhearing his pathetic patter. Fortunately, it seemed his efforts to persuade her fell into an unresponsive abyss of silence. Effy seemed to be in some world of her own. Whatever was happening in her head, I had no idea. I choose to believe she was engaged in some personal mental struggle with no intention of being seduced. Nor do I believe my arrival had anything to do with her decision. That's what I'd like to believe. But I guess what went through Effy's thoughts at the time will remain secret.

We now know Simon Silvers was up to no good. His attempt to seduce her was deliberate and planned. Worse still, he was the tool of others who had other separate mischiefs planned. Thankfully, Effy got over the emotional turmoil with our help and her sisters who rallied around her.

The Halloran girls had come from an Irish Catholic background with heavily prescribed attitudes. To find themselves in a profession where they were selling their bodies as moving mannequins did not go down well with their parents. Their professional lives proved trying at times. A few photographers we had to work with had womanising reputations, and the odd one or two sordid expectations. I think I surprised Ellen Halloran one day. She found me punching seven bells out of a well-known fashion snapper. His attempt to take liberties with me ended badly after he lured me into a side room. The black eye was a beauty. His backside planted on the floor would remind him never to mess with me again. Hopefully not with other models either. Ellen could not stop cackling as she took in what I had done to him.

I think the sight of me knocking a man to the floor impressed Ellen. She had already experienced one rape attempt while still in the Sixth Form. As for fifteen-year-old Grace? We had our work cut out, keeping grubby paws off her body. Lolita age girls with gamine bodies constantly attracted the wrong kind of attention. Many of the men were in their mid to late twenties. Some were older, all of whom ought to have known better. We had to chaperoned Grace to all shoots until she was eighteen, as we did with Joy Heatherington, too. Safety in numbers became an agency priority for those under eighteen.

I suppose my experiences as a man moulded my perceptions as a woman. The instinct to protect these young girls came naturally as I increasingly understood how the male world viewed them and me. I was ready to defend the girls in our agency against any attempts to use or abuse them to satisfy some man's sexual fantasies. We had learned valuable lessons with Devane.

The problems women now experienced had coincided with the arrival of The Pill. Once women had The Pill, their world and reality changed. I watched it happen. Men saw themselves freed from the responsibility for taking care of contraception. They assumed all women now took care of the birth control thing. Therefore, women were now fair game for indiscriminate sexual encounters. Therein lay the problem.

Men came to regard single women who slept around as promiscuous slags. Those women who didn't sleep around were contemptuously called frigid. It was a no-win situation for women, many of whom were only looking for love and a decent man. Each would be Alfie could make and break a woman's reputation one way or another. It was fine for men to sow their wild oats but not for a woman. To do the same as men was to earn an unwarranted reputation. They had to bear the consequences if things went wrong.

Where having a child was concerned women still also faced judgments. Women were stigmatised if they had a baby outside of marriage, or as a teen. If they married but didn't have a child, they were also stigmatised. As for having an abortion? This came with the ultimate stigma if ever revealed.

Sexual freedom for many young women still clashed with the desire to find the man of their dreams. Ones who played the field, like Hester, experiencing a short-lived euphoria. Unfettered sexual licence, even power over men, soon led to realising how emotionally empty and unfulfilling sleeping around could become. Respect for young women appeared to be at a new low within a short period.

As The New Breed, we enjoyed a degree of immunity from predatory males. The young women who signed up with the Agency came to regard it as a haven. Most of the top photographers generally behaved themselves when they hired us. Not that we didn't still get the occasional stories of unsolicited wandering hands or invitations to share a bed. These continued to remain an issue with some, although Mack's reputation as our guardian worked in our favours. Mention of his name was often enough to elicit good behaviour. For an eighteen-year-old, Mack's reputation proved truly scary as events in 1968 proved.

Tales of his penchant for chilling violence, though greatly exaggerated, acquired a kind of frightening mythic quality after New York. The way he punished members of *Zorro's Mask* rock group has become the stuff of legend. The encounters with Konstantinos also became public despite Henderson's best efforts to suppress them. The Konstantinos Affair still remains something of an unsolved mystery.

Harry Crawford's autobiographical account of his fight with Mack at Bethnal Green boxing club has further contributed to the legend. In more recent biographies, Mack's street-fighting man credentials have received undue attention. So too has his so-called connection with the Maltese underworld in London. Sometimes in life there are no choices, he once told me. You have to do what you have to do. In life there are no Queensbury rules. He was right. There are none, as Jack Torrance, Harry Crawford, Nikos Konstantinos, and others learned to their cost.

When it comes to photographic creativity and technical ingenuity, Mack MacKinnon ranks among the best. His vision and creative magic remain remarkable.

Mack always loved the idea of taking photos that appeared as if they were stills from a movie. A photographed scene had to capture a significant emotional moment in a narrative. In this way, he not only captured the fashion, but he also turned the shots into something far more artistically and culturally meaningful. I think the idea of directing movies began with his kind of photography. Although, I believe his friend, *Jersey*, Anton Dzerzhinsky, was the one who encouraged him to use his talent in that direction.

The truth is Mack's reputation as a talented professional drew top models to him. What he accomplished with us in the New Breed, he knew he could do with others, and not only with models. Movie stars, starlets, pop singers, rock groups, writers, politicians, and any newsworthy celebrity could benefit from his vision behind the lens. However, his meteoric rise to fame was, and remains, tied to his remarkable way with women. He understood them, and they understood him. Most loved him for his approach and the ability to make them feel good about themselves and to look even better when photographed. His spectacular photographic results have featured in more than a few autobiographies and articles. His remarkable photography continues to stand the test of time.

Chapter 29

Respect – Aretha Franklin (Atlantic AT 584115 – 1967)

Undated.

"Who knows what women can be when they are finally free to be themselves."
Betty Friedan

I never burned my bra, as some women insisted on doing. My bras were not the cheap kind anyway. I could never see the point of being wasteful for a gesture.

Alice was born to have a tiny bust and long legs, which I no choice but to inherit. These attributes made my modelling career a runaway success. Flat chested boyish figures with long legs were in demand. Like Jane Birkin, I often never bothered to wear a bra at all. So, what if my nipples showed through my clothes? They were a sign of my femininity, and I was not ashamed to have them showing.

My interest in the Women's Lib movement had a certain inevitability. Given my unusual perspective, this can hardly be surprising. In my lifetime as a man, I had held the attitudes typical of the men of my generation. Only after experiencing life as a young woman did, I relate to the inequalities confronting women.

Money remains the great liberator. That is a fact of life. It will never change as long as wealth inequalities exist.

My financial independence was secured by my choice of career and a meteoric rise to fame. As an international fashion model, my work provided me with the kind of earning power few women could ever hope to attain. Yet, my financially secure life could so easily have tempted me to deny the inequalities experienced by most women.

In the late Sixties, male attitudes continued to remain dominant despite the apparent changes. Men still believed themselves pre-eminent. Token advancement happened in some professions, but true equality then, as we understand it now, did not yet exist. This made life difficult for women aspiring to reach the top in their chosen fields. It happened in nearly all walks of life too. Effy's sister, Deidre, who qualified as a doctor, found the going tough in what was still essentially a male-dominated medical profession. To qualify as a surgeon proved an even tougher challenge.

The times did not change with the arrival of the so-called permissive Swinging Sixties. Men still regarded themselves as the providers, while women continued to be viewed as the domestic and submissive other halves. Understandably, I had no intention of conforming to any male patriarchal expectations. The only men who had earned my complete respect were James MacKinnon, his father Robert, and Nate. To a lesser extent, maybe Eugene Henderson, who understood talent in business had no gender. Hence his bizarre retention of Pearl Piper's services despite her methods.

Having been a man, I knew what it meant to be one. As a woman, I now also knew women did not want to emulate men. Why would we? As for liberation? What did that mean? The right to have the same kinds of freedom as any man? That at the least, certainly. More importantly, what women wanted, and still do, is respect.

Aretha Franklin's version of *Respect* had sent more than a shiver through my person on first hearing. Men have mentally and physically enslaved women with their patriarchal attitudes for as long as historical records had existed. These attitudes needed, and still need, to change. The simple truth is, we don't want to emulate men, nor do we want to adopt a masculine role. To do so would not be true equality nor true liberation. It would cost us our womanhood.

Back in the Sixties, the word sexism did not yet exist, although the idea already did. Male superiority in all aspects of life had been seen as unreasonable and unacceptable for a long time. Some women knew even then in the Sixties that it would take a lifetime and more to rid the world of sexist attitudes. Decades later, sexism remains, and the battle against it is far from over. I suspect it may never be totally eradicated. Certainly not until religions cease their disgusting and contemptuous doctrines enabling men to repress women. Religions remain an anathema, wholly unacceptable, and not only for their sexist theologies.

It wasn't just the constant sexual harassment experienced in daily life that affected me. The leering eyes you encountered on the street, men trying to look up your skirt when you went upstairs on a bus or an escalator. Or suddenly finding a sly hand on your behind while travelling on a crowded tube in the rush hour. Or yet another *accidentally on purpose* touch in a crowded store. Or worse still, the unwanted pathetic approaches made by strange men with invitations to go back to their place. No. Incidents of this kind were never acceptable behaviour. Nor were the ways we found ourselves treated by men as childishly inept pretty little things.

I can still recall the supercilious grin that greeted me in a car dealership. The conversation that followed angered me almost to rage. Imagine my reaction and how I felt hearing these outrageous words: perhaps, Madam should come back with your boyfriend / fiancé / husband / father? Technical specifications can be so tricky and confusing for you young ladies. Or the one that rankled most of all, when I tried to obtain a mortgage. I am so sorry, *dear*. Single women are not allowed mortgages. Come back with your fiancé/husband so we can discuss the matter. I left spitting venomous comments in his ears. Yet, there were moments of triumph too. Like seeing the estate agent's expression when I purchased my first home in Kensington for cash as a twenty-two-year-old woman.

There were downsides to becoming famous. You became a celebrity as your fame grew. Then the press expected you to become a part of the celebrity circus.

When Harry Crawford's attempts to date Angie failed, he turned his attentions unsuccessfully to me. It didn't stop with him. Once you were even vaguely famous, you became a target for every male with a hard on. More so if you were also pretty and wearing a mini skirt. I came to understand how this could make you feel demeaned. You saw yourself as nothing more than a trophy to be won by some bloke in a pop group. If not him, then some film star, or some millionaire, or possibly a titled aristocrat of either foreign or domestic pedigree. Fortunately, my life as a man had prepared me for this.

In my new life, I belonged to a group of young women who were a breed apart. We looked after one another and never became pushovers for predatory men and suitors. What more needs saying?

Every one of the women in the New Breed has meant the world to me. I treasure each one of them, and the experiences we shared together as women. For their friendships, I am deeply grateful. They helped to make me the woman I wanted to become.

I admire each of them for the different ways in which they asserted themselves.

Angie Thornton, we remain the closest of friends. Our daughters are not only half-sisters but best friends. For me, you will always be the strongest-willed and most determined woman I have ever met. One who would square up to any man in business meetings without giving an inch. Sometimes it meant a loss of business, but our services and models were the best of any agency, and the corporate men knew it. Angie, you earned grudging respect from them for your methods. Your refusal to be used in your career as a film actor was another object lesson for young women to follow. What a shame you gave up acting so soon. You were born to be a movie star and could have been a great one.

Grace, when you took over running Effy's fashion empire, you proved equally creative and adept in your dealings. Nor did you lack business acumen or toughness. Your softer edge masked the toughness beneath. Much of what you learned in dealing with men you acquired from Angie and Hester. What a pity you have not been more discriminating about the men in your personal life. At least you're an expert on dealing with them.

Effy Halloran, what a talent you are. Not just a fashion designer, a model, and a businesswoman, you are an artist who has sketched and painted truly amazing works of art. I applaud the decision you took to step down from your fashion business to raise your family. You are the most generous and open-hearted woman I have ever known. Mack is so lucky to have you. I look forward to seeing the novels I know you are writing.

Dear Ellen. We always worked brilliantly together. You should have become a teacher like you always wanted. Instead, you founded the New Breed Modelling Academy as an extension of our agency. Thanks to your efforts, you have schooled younger generations of successful models. Like Effy, you made Tom and your children your priority.

Sara Silvers, under Mack's guidance and wholehearted encouragement, you achieved your ambition. You became a top fashion photographer in the Seventies. Like your brother Nate, you had common sense, acumen, and a love of others. You have built strong friendships among us. What an asset you became for The New Breed.

Hester, my dear, dear friend, you were always destined to run *Mystique*. Your father had it planned from the start. When you succeeded your mother, Celia, you took the magazine into new markets. Today *Mystique* remains one of the premier international fashion magazines. It will stay like this while ever you are at the helm. Your father was always proud of you and had the vision to see your abilities and potential.

I am proud of you all for proving yourselves. I am proud of you for helping other girls and young women to prove themselves. I want you all to know how much I love and respect you.

Simone de Beauvoir's quote has haunted me ever since I first came across her words. *One is not born, but rather becomes, a woman.* We become who

144

we are by the choices we make. As a man, I found myself shaped by the world of my lifetime, its expectations of me, and the choices then open to me. As a woman, rightly or wrongly, I was expected to conform to the gender expectations of previous generations. The fact that I became who I am made the expectations problematic.

The more I reflect on the duality of my existence, the more I am driven to one conclusion: we are not born anything, not male, not female. We become fashioned by gender assumptions at birth as much as by our biological differences, as well as the times in which we live. My new gender came unexpectedly and without warning. I became a woman not by choice but by supernatural or preternatural intervention. Living my life for so long as Alice, I barely feel a connection anymore between Phil Manley and who I am now. Some days I wonder if I was ever him, or if he is a fiction of my imagination. Time has made him seem unreal. As for my life as Alice? My good fortune was to be reborn a young woman of the swinging Sixties.

The young women around me during the Sixties saw themselves living in a time of sweeping changes. Like me, they decided not to conform to expected norms. Cultural and social upheavals transformed our attitudes towards the way we lived our lives. In doing so, we hoped everything would change. It didn't. For the most part, we women are still on the journey to true equality. At least some positive changes did happen because of the awareness created by the Women's Lib movement. All that bra-burning proved to be so much more than empty gestures.

Chapter 30

Que Sera, Que Sera (Whatever Will be, Will Be) – The High Keys
(London HLK 9768 -1963)

Undated

Years ago, I came across a line in a novel that decided me on motherhood. I wrote it down and fortuitously found it again going through my shambolic collection of diaries and notebooks. It came from a novel written by Margaret Attwood. If I wrote it down correctly it read like this: *no woman has fulfilled her femininity until she had had a baby.*

Motherhood created the most transforming change in my life as Alice. I have never been the same from the moment I knew I was pregnant. No one could have forewarned me, not in my wildest imaginings, how powerful the attachment to my daughter would become. Okay, it's supposed to be that way, I imagine most people thinking. It's what nature intended for us and hardwired it into our female DNA. The survival of our species depends on this imperative. We need to establish an enduring bond with the child we bring forth from our womb. Whether we like it or not, women are hi-jacked by this tiny new life growing inside them. This little bundle will be our joy and our ball and chain for the remainder of our lives, no matter what joy or grief their life brings to us.

Though I have never entirely lost my male memories, I am sure of one thing. My paternal responses to Cathy were never as strong as my maternal responses to Hester, my female-born daughter. That is not to say I don't love Cathy as much. Though I do admit, my new life has altered our relationship. How could it not? We became more like sisters after I became Alice. In both instances, my children are never far from my thoughts.

In some ways, I don't envy men at all. Not now I've lived as a woman and as a mother. Men never experience the bond of parenthood in quite the same way we women do. Of course, not all women are the same. In some, the maternal instinct is not as strong as in others. In me, it has been an all-powerful force. I'm fortunate my daughter Hester and I have always been close. So, I'm happy to say she will be my companion on our journey to find and finally meet the Alice who was. I know her half-sisters and brother will miss her badly, as will her father. Mack has been a devoted dad to my Hester

146

as he has to all her half-sisters and half-brother. One day she will return to you all, I promise. In the meantime, she insists on taking this journey with me.

Unresolved issues have confronted me for years. My need to learn how I died and became Alice has never been satisfactorily answered. Maybe it never will. Still, I want to try to find an answer since continuing conjectures serve no useful purpose. One thing has become apparent. The soul is not the body, nor is the body the soul.

As a man, I had lived in a different body into middle age. When my body died, I lived on in this new body along with my previous life's memories. Though these have faded and become distant with the passage of time, they have remained, even if with a faint and unreal dreamlike quality. Since then, this life as Alice has given me an insight into how men and women are different. Yet, like a coin, the two are inseparable sides differing only in the way we perceive each side.

For years after becoming Alice Liddell, I lacked the courage to ask the obvious question. Why me? Why had I become Alice? As Alice, I lived for a long time with uncertainty. I wondered if my new life could be blinked out in an instant without warning. Would I cease to exist? Would Alice return? What would happen? In a sense, my strange situation led me to consciously decide to live life as fully as I knew how. Once I adapted to being Alice, life blossomed.

When I questioned my existence as her, I also questioned the unfairness of the universe. My conclusion has been simple. The universe is a cruel place without pity. Something supernatural deprived Alice of her life and family to give me another life and family. Yet instinctively, somewhere in my depths, I have always suspected Alice did not die. That she too travelled on into a new life, as had I. Naturally, I had no proof, only a forlorn hope she had been reborn somewhere. Questioning in this way eventually led me to explore the ideas and theories surrounding reincarnation and rebirth. This is why I turned to writing novels dealing with reincarnation, as well as my more serious work: *The Transmigration of Souls*. Writing for me became a way of understanding if my strange lives served some higher purpose? The question has always been for what purpose?

Was my strange rebirth a singular cosmic accident? Or am I proof that we never truly die? Do we shed our bodies when they wear out in exchange for new ones? If so, are our bodies little more than transient organic abodes fit for single lifetimes? Are we, as Buddhists believe, destined to experience different lives as a mind in whatever lives we find ourselves? Which leads to even more complex philosophical questions. Is the mind the same as the soul, assuming the latter exists? If not, what is the difference?

The mind we are told resides in the brain and is our consciousness. It encompasses all that we are, how we think, reason, plan, apply and create. It is the source of our memories, imagination, and emotions, giving us our identity in physical life. As for the soul, that too has its questions? What is the soul?

Is the soul the divine and spiritual embodiment of the self as claimed by some religions? Does the soul also include the mind? Some theologies hold that when we die, the soul separates to reside in an afterlife. What kind of afterlife now appears to me to be a new life elsewhere in a new body. Which in turn leads me to other questions.

The journey from one body to the next, is this part of a supernatural act beyond our understanding? Or is it a preternatural evolutionary process we have yet to understand scientifically? Are there finite limits to a soul's cyclical journeying? If so, what is the end purpose of such journeying? There are so many more questions to which I want the answers. Or at the very least, I want to know why it happened to me?

Thus far, my life as Alice has been fortunate and exceptional. It has been a life lived for my daughters, the Liddell's, my close friends, and for me. Now, I have a journey to undertake. This time it will be without you, my family, and friends. Perhaps, one day, someday in the future, we will come together once more. If not, remember my love is with you all, always. Know I am secure in myself, knowing who I have been. Which, if it means anything at all now, means little. A name is a label. And labels can never tell the whole tale. So let me leave you with a quote to ponder.

"'Be what you would seem to be.' — Or, if you'd like it put more simply—'Never imagine yourself not to be otherwise than what it might appear to others that what you were or might have been was not otherwise than what you had been would have appeared to them to be otherwise.'"

Lewis Carroll
Chapter 9,
The Mock Turtle's Story.
(Alice in Wonderland)

Afterword

When I spoke to my sister-in-law, Catherine Liddell née Manley, she was reluctant to speak about Alice or her father. I gave her a copy of Alice's manuscript to read. Even after reading the manuscript, Catherine refused to say anything to me about the contents. She smiled and said we should remember Alice for who Alice was and the kind things she did.

In the past, I often wondered how and why Alice and Cathy had become such close friends. It made no sense at the time. The two were strangers yet seemed to know one another like lifelong friends. I found their close relationship strange. Alice attended Crossley & Porter, while Cathy went to Princess Mary's. Added to that, they lived on opposites sides of the town. In the manuscript, Alice wrote I was suspicious of the way their friendship had started. She was right. That is a memory I distinctly recollect and can verify. Yes, the two were curiously close. Their relationship was unusual and different from the one Alice shared with Angie Thornton or Hester Clayton. I remember thinking Alice seemed almost maternal towards Cathy. If her father's mind had displaced my sister's, then so much of what I read makes sense.

The answer, I believe, lies in a copy of Phil Manley's death certificate that Angie Thornton obtained. She pointed out the significant pieces of information to me. The dates not only tallied but so too did the changes that took place in Alice. According to her own words, it was all too coincidental not to be true.

As I read the manuscript, many other things made sense. The inexplicable changes to Alice's personality at the time. Most strikingly of all, how she became almost an instant adult after returning from the hospital. Also, her arguments with our mother about going to see the psychiatrist. (I can clearly remember those happening and the fuss she kicked up about the visits). We thought they were due to her amnesia and a need to compensate for her memory loss. Now, thinking back to those times, Alice's words explain so much more.

When Alice revived, she was nothing like the sister I knew. It was as though she was a stranger, someone who had become another person. If Alice was indeed Phil Manley. then it explains her paternal efforts to ensure we were all provided for in life. The more I reflect on what she did for us, the more her actions have been wholly caring and unselfish. She bought my mother a lovely new house and paid all her bills. When Frank married, this allowed him to take over our old home on Ivy Street. Alice even bought him a family car big enough to cope with three children and his wife. There were always plenty of presents on birthdays and at Christmas for everyone in the family. She also gave my mother the gift of a beautiful and talented granddaughter. I delight in being an aunt to a gorgeous and loving niece.

For myself, I have her to thank for my higher education. Alice paid for my time at university both as an undergraduate and as a post-graduate. Harvard was an expensive school to attend. Then there were the numerous paid-for foreign holidays to broaden my horizons and fashionable clothes to fill my wardrobes. Alice made sure I never went short of anything, nor any of my family. My sister is a loving person. Whoever she claims she was, she will always be Alice*, my sister.

Amen.

Edie Liddell

*Alice. Meaning of name. Truth, reality.

All about *Alice* – The author's apology.

Let me tell you a secret. I didn't choose to write *Alice*. The novel chose me. If you don't find that strange, you will understand what I'm trying to say. The idea for Alice's story had haunted me for some years. Long before I introduced her as a character in the 1967 trilogy, I knew who she would be and the part she would play.

As I wrote the story, I jokingly referred to *Alice* as my Kafkaesque novel. Unlike Kafka, I prefer to write fiction of an uplifting nature. Dark themes have never attracted me. I leave that kind of writing to others. Hence, I hope Phil Manley's journey into a new life as Alice will be seen as an uplifting tale.

I further hope Lewis Carroll fans take no exception to my use of his work as a leitmotif. Since he wrote *Alice in Wonderland,* generations have enjoyed this wonderful tale. Unlike Lewis Carroll's story, I never intended to make *Alice* fantastical, nor could I.

There are references to other authors in the novel, Virginia Woolf and Gore Vidal, for which I make no apologies. These writers wrote about similar or related themes, and they clearly had some bearing on my writing.

As I jotted down my ideas for the novel, I knew I needed to draw together a number of themes relating to the Jimmy Mack Sixties saga/series. After all, Alice was always intended to be a book in the ongoing series.

My choice of The Sixties as a decade was not simply as a historical setting or backdrop. The Sixties remain emblematic, a symbol of a time of social and cultural changes. The change brought about by The Pill empowered women, but not without consequences. Sexism was then and has continued to remain a disturbing problem within many societies in the world. Men may be sympathetic, but they are not always empathetic about what happens to women and girls in their daily lives. Put in their position, men and boys would soon see the world differently.

Alice becoming a Mod was integral to her teenage identity and her part in the saga. The Mod subculture was a distinct youth movement visible on the streets of Sixties Britain and in keeping with the fast-moving social changes as they occurred. While Mods may have had a passion for fashion and they were all about having a good time all the time, they were aspirational young people at heart. Something for nothing was never an option for them. Most implicitly understood, if you wanted anything out of life, you had to be prepared to work to get it.

Today, the Sixties Generation X are retired and in the twilight of their lives. Many became achievers in their respective walks of life. Nor have many of these original Sixties Mods forgotten their young adult roots. They have remained Mods at heart. For them, the saying, *once a Mod always a Mod*, still remains true. For many of them, their youth has also remained the best of times.

Acknowledgements

First and foremost, I am indebted to Bill Williams, my friend, and long-time neighbour in Spain. Even though ninety, Bill loved to discuss many of the ideas being raised in the novel. We had endless laughs as well as more serious and stimulating philosophical debates. I am grateful to him for the times we spent over *té ingles* and *tartas* chatting about the questions the novel posed.

As always, include my dear wife, Julie. She is my soulmate, and we are one another's rocks. Without her, none of my writing would be possible. We share our trials and tribulations as one.

I want to thank so many kind friends and readers who have supported me one way or another during a tremendously difficult time in our lives as I worked to complete the novel. In no particular order: Natalie Finnigan, Graham Wilkinson, Paul Hooper-Keeley, Karen Keeley, Kevin Bagnall, Susan Smith, Kathryn Magson, Nikki & Andy Topp-Walker, Kai Ahland, Vanessa & Tony Beesley, Jason Brummell, Jayne Thomas, Johnny Bradley, Mickey Danby-Foy, Mark Aldridge, Carl & Deborah Blackburn, Michael Grogan, Les Roberts, Jane George, Helen-Claire O'Connor, Dave Varley, Bill Williams, and Richard Newsome. Also, anyone who has supported me on Facebook, Instagram, or Twitter.

If I've missed anyone I apologise.

A big thank you to all who have bought and read my books.

The Soundtrack

Chapter 1
We'll Meet Again – Vera Lynn (Decca F.7268 – 1939)

Chapter 2
If I Could Live My Life – Dorothy Price (MPAC 7206 – 1963)

Chapter 3
Can't Get Used To Losing You – Andy Williams (CBS AAG 138 – 1963)

Chapter 4
Why Can't A Woman Be More Like A Man? – Rex Harrison
(My Fair Lady - Original Soundtrack CBS SBRG 72237 LP 1964)

Chapter 5
Good Morning Little Schoolgirl – The Yardbirds (Columbia DB7391 – 1964)

Chapter 6
Walk - Don't Run '64 – The Ventures (Liberty LIB 96 – 1964)

Chapter 7
You Can Make It If You Try – Yvonne Fair/James Brown (King 45-5687 – 1962)

Chapter 8
Get A Job – The Silhouettes (Parlophone R4407 – 1968)

Chapter 9
In My Life – The Beatles (Rubber Soul LP. Parlophone PMC 1267 – 1965)

Chapter 10
Reflections – The Supremes (Tamla Motown TMG 616 –1967)

Chapter 11
I Don't Need No Doctor – Ray Charles (HMV POP 1566 – 1966)

Chapter 12
Sho 'Nuff Got A Good Thing Goin' – J.J. Jackson (Warner Bros WB 2082 – 1967)

Chapter 13
Living To Please – Dolores Clark feat. Ray Starling (Antares AX 101 – 1966)

Chapter 14
The Human Jungle – John Barry 7 & Orchestra (Columbia DB7003 – 1963)

Chapter 15
So What? – Bill Black Combo (London HLU 9594 – 1962)

154

JIMMY MACK – SOME KIND OF WONDERFUL

The drug fuelled all-night Mod dance scene of the Sixties is the backdrop to a secret love. Soul music, the soundtrack to this intense love affair.

You're never too young to fall in love. Some things are just meant to be. A wink outside church one Sunday brings Fiona "Effy" Halloran into James "Mack" MacKinnon's life. It's 1964 in the West Riding of Yorkshire. For the two fifteen-year-olds the next two years will prove a test of their love and devotion to one another.

Growing up is never easy, nor is being young and in love. When Effy's sister Caitlin becomes pregnant by Mack's brother the lives of their families collide. Dealing with a feuding family, itself divided by religious zeal, becomes a serious obstacle for the young lovers. Separated by circumstances can their love for one another survive?

Over time Mack and Effy learn the truth about their respective families because secrets never stay secret forever.

Jimmy Mack - Some Kind of Wonderful" is the first of a series of novels set in Bradford and Halifax between 1964 and 1969 involving the twosome and their friends. Parallel interweaving novels in the same time period are in the process of being written.

"...this is a beautiful book. I couldn't wait to finish it and now I'm sad I have as I want more. It is a great journey through teenage life and love that we have all been a part of. I LOVE IT!"

"I absolutely love Jimmy Mack. Nostalgia, rite of passage and fashion and music. You covered it all. I am sad I finished it. I cannot wait for the next one."

Amazon Reviews

★★★★★

AVAILABLE ONLINE FROM:
Feed A Read. (feedaread.com) and Amazon.
ISBN-10: 1788760433 / ISBN-13: 978-1788760430

JIMMY MACK 1967 – STRONG LOVE (SIDE A)

THE FIRST NOVEL IN THE 1967 TRILOGY.

Mack, Effy and Angie are three smart, sharp and stylish young Mods in search of a future. Soul music and the all-night dance scenes of Halifax, Bradford and Manchester's famed Twisted Wheel club are the backdrop to their lives.

Mack and Effy's love affair is intense and torrid. Angie is their best friend, but she and Mack share a secret they can never reveal to Effy. As 1967 unfolds their lives change forever. A fateful encounter at Angie's eighteenth birthday party will take the three to London.

When a soured drug deal resurfaces Mack's past catches up with him, sparking revenge and violence.

Their passion for fashion opens a door in Chelsea's King's Road to fledgling careers. London's Swinging Sixties nightlife will bring them before the full glare of the press. Are their dreams about to come true? Or will Mack and Angie's secret destroy everything?

This novel will surprise and challenge reader's understanding of love and friendship.

Jimmy Mack 1967 – Strong Love (Side A) is the first part of the 1967 trilogy and the second in the Jimmy Mack Series. The trilogy follows on from the opening novel of the forthcoming Jimmy Mack series.

"What a story. I was intrigued throughout. The twists and turns. Great writing. I have also written a review on both books on Amazon. Can't wait for the next book."

Graham Wilkinson
Amazon
★★★★★

"Wonderful books - I enjoyed them both tremendously. Highly recommended."

Paul Hooper-Keeley

ONLINE FROM: Feed A Read. (feedaread.com) and Amazon.
OR FROM YOUR LOCAL BOOKSHOP QUOTING: ISBN: 9781788765534

JIMMY MACK 1967 – LET THE GOOD TIME ROLL (SIDE B)

THE SECOND NOVEL IN THE 1967 TRILOGY.

What happens when fame and fortune come calling?

Mack, Effy and Angie find instant success in the fashion world of the 1960s. But nothing is straightforward or simple. This is a love story with a difference.

What if the three are two couples?
Effy and Angie are best friends who have agreed to share Mack living life as two separate couples.

Their new lives will take the three away from the North of England and the Mod scene thrusting them into high earning celebrity careers. As their fame grows, they will find themselves in London, Spain and New York.

Along the way they will experience press and fashion industry intrigue, deception and malice.

Can their unusual love arrangement survive?

"Another masterpiece from the pen of John Knight. I love the uncertainty of the plot. Got totally caught up in the story and had so many different feelings towards the end of the book. Yet I know it's only a novel. Without trust you've got nothing. What else can I say? Brilliant."

Graham Wilkinson
Amazon

★★★★★

"I waited for this book with both excitement and trepidation. Could it be as good? I needn't have worried because Let The Good Times Roll surpassed all expectations."

K.S. Bagnall
Amazon

★★★★★

AVAILABLE ONLINE FROM: Feed A Read. (feedaread.com) and Amazon: ISBN:9781839450716

JIMMY MACK 1967 – THE NEW BREED

THE THIRD NOVEL IN THE 1967 TRILOGY.

LONDON CALLING…

…And James 'Mack' MacKinnon and The New breed collective are answering
the call. Touted as the new teen David Bailey he and his models are setting the
fashion world alight.

Effy Halloran's disappearance haunts him and Angie his other girlfriend.
Why did the young talented designer disappear after their return from New York?
Her disappearance is set for more intrigue and deception as he searches for answers.

Who is Joy Heatherington? And how will her arrival change their lives?
His search for answers in Chelsea and Soho will unearth more than he
bargained for.

"Another masterpiece from the pen of John Knight. I love the uncertainty of the plot. Got totally
caught up in the story and had so many different feelings towards the end of the book. Yet I
know it's only a novel. Without trust you've got nothing. What else can I say? Brilliant."

Graham Wilkinson
Amazon
★★★★★

"I waited for this book with both excitement and trepidation. Could it be as good? I needn't
have worried because Let The Good Times Roll surpassed all expectations."

K.S. Bagnall.
Amazon
★★★★★

AVAILABLE ONLINE FROM: Feed A Read. (feedaread.com) and Amazon
ISBN:978-1-83945-531-5

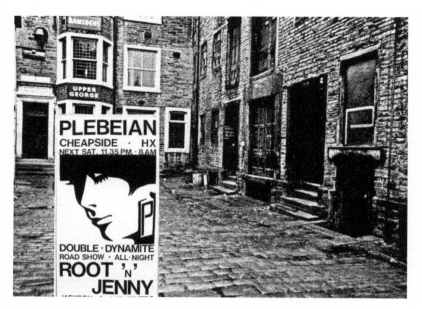

The Upper George Yard. Pub & Plebeians club (R), February 1966.

CROSSLEY & PORTER GRAMMAR SCHOOL

The Author

Lightning Source UK Ltd.
Milton Keynes UK
UKHW011824281021
393005UK00001B/60